Scion

DRAGONS OF THE CROSSROADS BOOK 3

LORI SALTIS

VAGABOND TALES

I dedicate this book to Andy Pettit.
Thank you for your friendship and hospitality through the years. You know the best places to live.

Lennon

I spend the night of my eighteenth birthday with the girl of my dreams.

Nothing happens. Nothing can happen.

But that's okay.

Lying in bed with Penny cuddled against me is the best birthday present I could ask for, especially given my current circumstances, which are sucktastic to say the least. In theory, I'm the Dragon Son, head of the Two Dragon Clan. In reality, I'm a punk kid who pissed off a lot of powerful people, and those people want payback. The only thing stopping them is that I'm powerful, too, and a dragon has my back. Sort of. Actually, he's kind-of a dick. The dragon, I mean, but that's how dragons are, I guess. I've only met the one.

Penny stirs against me as she blinks and yawns. That does… things to me and I shift away. She stares up at me with eyes like twin emeralds. Her smile is like being slapped by the sun. I'm dazzled and my body burns. I want the world to go away so I can spend my life in this room, in her bed, being scorched by her sunshine. Her rosebud mouth becomes a wide cavern as she yawns and stretches. She rises on her forearms and gives a soft groan before murmuring, "So sleepy." She collapses onto her pillow, grumbling as she tugs the bedding up to her chin, and closes her eyes.

Tenderness wells up in my chest. I've always felt tender toward Penny, but right now it's overwhelming. I want to kiss her - I mean, really kiss her, with tongues and stuff, but I also don't want to. It's hard to explain. I love Penny and want to be with her in, you know, that way, but also, she's my friend - my best friend - and I don't want that to change. It feels like a single touch could change everything and I'm not ready for that, so I ease out of bed. I'm not leaving, not without saying goodbye, but there's someone I need to talk to. Using Silent Steps so not to wake her, I glide to the large window leading out to the fire escape and lift it open. Before stepping out, I glance back at Penny.

Ah, dear Juliet, why art thou yet so fair?

A chill shudders through me. My knees go weak. In my junior year, I had to write a report about Romeo and Juliet. The whole time, I thought about me and Penny. We're not from opposing families. Strowlers and the Two Dragon Clan have little interaction, but our love is forbidden as if we were from Verona. I won't be Romeo finding Juliet in her tomb. Nothing bad will happen to her because of me.

Dew coats the fire escape and drips off the lawn chair and tomato plants on the small, makeshift balcony. Thick fog shrouds the sky and obscures the nearby buildings, so I feel like I'm suspended on a tiny island in the air. Mist clings to my skin and dampens my T-shirt and jeans. I like being out here like this. It feels like the real world doesn't exist. Other worlds, and the other otherworldly, seem more possible.

Hey, Ancestor, are you nearby? Can we talk?

I scan San Francisco from the bay to the ocean. Nothing. On an impulse, I go southeast. There's a story among the Asian communities that a huge dragon lies asleep beneath the San Francisco Bay, its head in the city, its tail in Milpitas, and that earthquakes happen when it shifts in its sleep. I find Jade Dragon in the southern end of the bay. He's shrunk to the size of an otter and swimming through the murky depths. My nose wrinkles. There's a sewage treatment plant nearby. How can he stand it? He burrows through silt to examine huge calcified tailbones submerged in the sludge. My heart sinks. The legend is true, but not in a good way. Jade Dragon once told me there were few dragons left. How few? Does he talk to me because he's lonely?

Did you know him? I ask.

Her, replies Jade Dragon. *No. She was one of the first, the Great Ones. She died before I spawned.*

How did she die?

She simply did. Her time had come, and she had no desire to leave the mortal world.

What does that even mean? If I ask, he'll answer with more cryptic bullshit. I'm better off trying to pry out answers that pertain to now. *So, speaking of other dragons, Penny told me she's descended from a dragon, too. His name is Master Stoorworm. You know him?*

Human names mean nothing, not even my own.

Okay, so, what's your dragon name?

His answer is a long stream of hisses and bubbles.

How do you say that in human?

Last Born of the Youngest He Shall Remain Until.

Until what?

Jade Dragon emerges from the silt and swims north toward colder, cleaner waters. I know from experience he won't answer the wrong question. I search for a right one.

Have you heard of another dragon that was messing around with humans or fairies, or whatever?

Last Born of the Eldest He Shall Remain Until.

I blink. Did he actually tell me something important? *Is that Master Stoorworm? Is Penny one of his descendants?*

If she says so, she is.

He rolls and splashes in the water until his scales are clean. Then he rises out of the Bay, becoming invisible as he grows in size to the length of a football field.

Where are you going?

Where I will go.

Wait. I need to ask you something else.

Jade Dragon hovers, undulating, stirring the surface of the water.

Did you know Tony was my dad's son?

Yes.

Of course, he did. Anger burns through my chest, interfering with our connection. I take a deep breath and restrain myself from shaking my fist and mentally yelling at him.

Why didn't you tell me?

What would you have done if I told you?

I don't know. I rub my frustration onto my forehead. *No one would've believed me if I'd told them about my invisible dragon friend, but maybe I could've lied and said I overheard Dad's confession or something.*

You learned the truth when those responsible confessed. Isn't that better?

No. It was a hell of a lot harder and involved a lot of suffering.

Yes. Good. Hatchlings must strive and suffer if they are to grow.

I'm not a fucking hatchling!

You are what you are.

And he's gone. See what I mean about him being a dick? Why can't he give me a straight answer? Because dragons don't help their young, which is probably why there aren't a lot of dragons left.

Did you ever think about that, genius?

There's a creak behind me as Penny leans out the window.

She's pulled on her long, chunky hand-knit sweater, which is a good idea since I don't need any reminders of how hot she is.

"Hey," she says with a puzzled squint. "You didn't hear Bridie?"

"No?" Shoot. That's the problem with talking to Jade Dragon. He commands your entire attention.

"She came in to say breakfast is ready. And to check on us." Her eyes roll.

Last night, Bridie was crazy happy when we told her that Tony is the actual Dragon Son and he and his wife can cure Matthew. She even allowed me to spend the night in Penny's room, as long as I swore on my honor to behave. Everyone seems to think all Penny and I want to do is jump each other's bones. I mean, yeah, but also, no. They don't get it. Nobody gets it but me and her.

"Were you talking to someone?"

I force myself not to blink. "Who would I talk to? I don't have my phone."

"I don't know. For some reason, I thought there was someone else out here." Her mouth spreads in a smirk. "Talking to yourself?"

I shrug like she caught me and I don't want to admit it. Had she sensed Jade Dragon? Or maybe I was talking aloud and didn't realize it.

Her arms fold, bunching the sweater into a thick wad across her chest as she steps aside to let me in. We stand in the middle of the room. I rub the back of my neck while she stares at her feet, which are super cute. She's got a different color nail polish on each toe. Her chest rises and falls as she looks up. Her eyes have gone from bright emerald to cautious jade. "You sleep okay?"

I shake my head. "Did you?"

"Not really. How's your lip?"

My tongue tests the crusty scab that's formed there after my grandfather punched me. "Hurts."

Her nose crinkles in the most adorable way possible. "Want me to kiss it and make it better?"

She doesn't have to ask twice. Our mouths touch, soft and sweet. The pain disappears. My heart spikes. I want to hold on to this moment forever. Words want to pour out of me about how awesome and glorious she is, but I'm afraid I'll spook her. Instead, I step back and hold out my hands. She takes them, twining her fingers with mine. I love her soft, cold hands and how her glitter-coated fingernails sparkle when they catch the light. I've noticed all this before but somehow now it all seems like magic. She squeezes tight and I squeeze back as if that could contain the feelings between us.

"So, breakfast," she says as she lets go.

I chew my lip and wince from the pain. "I can't. I have to go see Tony

Her smile fades as her teeth also go to work on her lip. "Are you sure he has the Yang Pearl?"

"I know he has it."

"I don't know who I feel worse for, you or him."

"Him," I say without hesitation. "And he's about to feel a lot worse."

"This sucks." She folds her arms again. "We don't have time for bad feelings or getting over it. Not any of us."

I don't want to go. I want to stay here, have breakfast and hang-out with nothing to do, like a normal teenager, like that's ever been a choice for me. "I have to go."

"How are you getting to the *kongsi*?"

Good question. If it was night, I could combine the flying and stealth skills to make my way across the city. During the day, even in the fog, it'd take more than my ability to make it all the way to Chinatown. I grin. "You think Bridie can give me a lift?"

She grins back. "Yeah, but you'd have to stay for breakfast. You don't have your bus pass?"

I shake my head. When Uncle George's goons grabbed me, they took everything on me.

Penny goes to her purse, pulls out her wallet and hands me the blue plastic card. "You can use mine."

"That'll work. I'll bring it back after I talk to Tony. And your phone."

"Okay. Promise?"

There's so much in that promise. All her family's best hopes. All my family's worst fears. I feel like I should say something, but I don't know what. Romeo would roll off some sick rhymes. All I can do is nod before saying, "I'll leave the way I came."

We go out to the fire escape and Penny sits on the lawn chair, folding her knees to her chest, as if she'll be waiting there until I return. Her painted nails give me those feelings, like I'd do anything for her and I have to turn away or I won't be able to leave.

I breathe in fog, letting it fill me, flow through me, and become part of me as I fade into its depths. Then I climb over the railing and fall to earth.

Penny

I blink and he's gone, and I release the breath I'm holding. It's like I want Lennon with me all the time, but when he's gone, I feel relieved because I can finally think straight. I rub my forehead as if scrubbing my brain. I can't believe my family's fate hinges on a pair of magic pearls gifted by a dragon. Most Strowler tales are facts wrapped in fancy to explain our mystical abilities. The Two Dragon Clan must be the same way, using a dragon to explain the inexplicable. Those pearls must be lodestones, attracting and storing power, the same way Strowlers use mirrors to seal and store our direst curse. A curse that reflects death. I shiver, like a goose walked over my grave. No, not my grave. Kingfisher's should that mirror ever break.

Sunlight shines through the fog and makes my nails shimmer. I wiggle my fingers and watch the glitter cast beams of refracted light. Something huge flies overhead, silent and casting no shadow. I shrink back, startled, before jumping up and scanning the sky. What the hell was that? Maybe a low-flying plane, its engine muffled by the fog. A vague sulphur scent lingers in the air before being blown away by the salty ocean breeze. I shiver again without benefit of goose or grave.

Then I go back inside and debate between sleep and coffee. Sleep wins.

For maybe ten minutes until Bridie bursts through the door and I'm startled out of a dream that flies away on reptile wings. I stare at her without raising my head.

She searches the room before meeting my gaze. "Where's Lennon?"

"He scarpered. Do that again and I'll go with him next time."

I roll over, away from her. Those words are as loaded as I meant them to be. Lennon will be here again and she can either trust me or I can leave. I'm eighteen and better educated than she was at my age. I feel her standing there, hand pressed to her chest, chewing her lip against saying the last word. The door clicks shut. I close my eyes, but my heart is pounding too hard and the ribbons of my dream have floated away. I rise with a deep sigh and head for the kitchen.

Both my coffee and oatmeal get dollops of cream and honey before I settle at the kitchen table. Kai is eating with one hand while tapping at his phone screen with the other.

"Where's Mum?" I ask.

"On the phone in the front parlor."

At this hour, calls are parents wanting to reschedule violins lessons or tenants whinging about a loose bit of carpet in the hallway. Whoever it is, Bridie will pour Charm into the receiver and the caller will hang up satisfied, regardless of whether she agreed to what they want.

"Where's Lennon?" he asks with a smirk.

"Gone."

"Without saying goodbye?"

"He blew you a kiss."

Kai scoffs and keeps tapping.

"How's Aaron?"

"Not good." He holds out his phone so I can see his friend's message.

Dude, Tony says he's totally not the Dragon
Son. Lennon is.

My spoon drops into my bowl as my stomach curls into a tight ball. "Yeah, well, Lennon says he needs to talk to Tony about it. He'll convince him." Bridie's footsteps sound in the hallway, so I finish with a whisper. "Don't tell Mum or she'll flip her shit."

"No shit," he whispers back.

Our mother enters the kitchen, clutching the phone to her chest. Dark circles bruise the delicate skin under her bloodshot eyes and her red hair is an unkempt tangle. Usually she looks younger than her age, but right now she looks ten years older. She pours herself a cup of coffee before settling at the table between me and Kai. "Matthew's parents called. Their house was ransacked last night. Fortunately, neither of them were there. They're afraid to go home now, so they're staying in the room across from Matthew. Charles told the care home he needs it for an incoming patient."

"Good idea." I say.

"Well, they're clever people, aren't they? Hopefully, clever enough to stay clear of that dreadful George Lau. Of course, they're terrified, but I assured them that Tony and May will be there soon with the Yang Pearl."

"That must've surprised them."

Bridie snorts. "Not at all. Enid has her sources, banished or no. She said the Two Dragon Clan's upheaval is good for us. All the chaos makes it easier for us to move freely."

My brow furrows. "No, it doesn't. Everything's a lot more chancy. I mean, we can't ask anyone for help because we don't know whose side they're on."

"I hadn't thought of that." She wrings her hands, a sure sign she's winding herself up. "Matty has no protection aside from his parents. Anyone could break into his room and steal the Yin Pearl and even kill him. We need help. Right now. I'll call Helena."

Having the Beggar Chief of London on our side should be a huge advantage, if it weren't also a way to call to call attention to ourselves with a bullhorn. As she reaches for her phone, I hold up my hand. "Wait. Let's think this through. George Lau doesn't know Matthew is alive. He doesn't even know for sure that the Wongs have the Yin Pearl. If the Beggar Clan starts lurking around the hospital, he'll get suspicious. That would put Matthew at a lot more risk."

Bridie covers her mouth. She speaks through her fingers. "We have to settle this right now. Where did you say Lennon went?"

"I didn't say, but he went to see Tony."

"Good lad. Get the ball rolling. I'm sure Tony will cooperate. He won't want you and Lennon shagging."

"Mum!" Kai covers his ears.

I roll my eyes, regretting not scarpering when I had the chance.

Bridie waves an impatient hand. "You and Lennon should be grateful having people look after your best interests. I couldn't stomach the thought of you being ruined over all this. Now, it's not our problem. Tony is the Dragon Son and he and his wife will deal with it."

Kai and I exchange uneasy glances. She doesn't know Tony like we do. Honor has made him rigid to the core. He can't bend without breaking. And then there's the matter of the Yang Pearl. How will he and Lennon get past that?

Lennon

Nothing makes you feel less badass than taking the bus. You can't own it like a boss when you arrive by public transportation and then have to ring the front doorbell because you don't have a key.

Joseph Alley is full of surveillance cameras, so I'm not surprised when Tony opens the door. He nods his single, manly nod. Mine in a mere head bob in comparison. I doubt I'll ever level up to the supreme masculinity that is his nod. I glance around the doorframe as I step inside. Yesterday, Jade Dragon blew open the front entrance so the Beggar Clan could storm the *kongsi* and rescue Penny. Today, nothing seems changed, except for the smell of scorched wood and fresh paint.

"That was fast," I say.

"We have the best people," Tony replies.

I sure hope so because we're going to need them. Members of the Two Dragon Clan are divided into three categories: craftsmen, warriors, and scholars. Craftsmen are the clan's blacksmiths, weapons makers, carpenters, and so on. Warriors are the muscle, meaning the fighters, spies, and security guards. Scholars are the brains of our outfit, the doctors, lawyers, financial advisors, and computer hackers. A great Dragon Son would have the skills of all three. A good Dragon Son should at least be a warrior and a scholar. I don't think I'm any of those things, which makes me feel more punk-ass than bad-ass right now.

We stop the front desk so I can pick up my phone, along with my keys and wallet. I look in the billfold. Everything is still there, but I know Head Elder and Uncle George can now use my ATM and credit card numbers to track my movements, which means I need to go to the bank.

"Where's Penny's phone?" I ask Tony.

"I had it delivered to her this morning."

Okay, that sounds nice, but I'm pretty sure that's his way of saying, 'so, you don't have an excuse to go see her.' Like we need an excuse. It's also a sign that Tony's shock has worn off, and he's not likely to drop me off at her place again anytime soon.

We're silent as we head upstairs. I brace myself, waiting for him to ask if I spent the night with her, but he doesn't. Does that mean he trusts me? I almost snort. No, it means he knows Bridie was enough of a watchdog to keep me and Penny apart.

Tony and his family live on the second floor, sort of. The *kongsi's* floors are numbered according to the Hong Kong standard, so what Americans call the first floor is the ground floor to us. The American second floor is our first floor and so on. This is to avoid admitting the *kongsi* is a four-story building, because to Chinese people, the number four is super bad luck. Think number thirteen on steroids.

We walk down the hall and pass his mother's shrine. Her diamond hard eyes follow us, demanding to know why there are no candles or incense lit and no fruit or flower offerings. I glare back at her. You think this is bad, lady, just you wait. You're about to be the hungriest ghost ever.

We enter the living room and Tony heads for his armchair while I settle cross-legged on the square leather ottoman. Even though I didn't call ahead, there's a teapot and a plate of ginger cookies on the coffee table. Tony's wife, May, is super thoughtful that way, but I also have to wonder if she realized she was setting an obstacle course. I reach over, fill a single cup and hold it out to Tony. He doesn't move. Our eyes lock. As the younger brother, I should pour and offer him the first cup, but if I'm the Dragon Son, he should do that for me, regardless of our ages. By offering him the cup, I'm not just acknowledging him as my older brother, but also as the Dragon Son.

Tony shakes his head. Of course he does. I knew it wouldn't be that simple. Hard-ass doesn't begin to describe how stubborn Tony can be, but I'm pretty stubborn, too. I shrug and take a sip. Why not? It's good tea with a delicate fragrance and goes down smooth, not like that bitter brew the Sparrows drink with their afternoon snack. I sigh before cramming a cookie in my mouth. May makes wonderful cookies. I love the chewy bits of crystalized ginger she uses.

He doesn't reach for a cookie. "I spoke at length with Second Elder last night. She and Fourth Elder managed to escape from Chisel Knife Mountain, along with others loyal to you."

The crumbs stick to my throat, glued there by guilt. I spent the night with my girlfriend and people's lives are on the line. I take a sip of tea so I can speak. "Where are they?"

"They've found refuge in the Mongkok *tong lau*."

"Really? That dump hasn't been knocked down yet?" It's an old school tenement building on Portland Street in Mongkok, one of the most densely populated places on earth. "Is it safe there?"

"It's in the heart of the Beggar Clan's territory. Now that Jeremiah Walks Long is head of the Crossroads, the entire

Beggar Clan supports you as Dragon Son. Brother Ash won't let anything happen to those loyal to you."

I met Brother Ash, the Beggar Chief of Hong Kong, on the day of the last Summoning Ceremony, when my father declared me his heir. He dressed in colorful rags and smoked a foul cigar to bug the shit out of the elite leaders of the Crossroads. I thought he was fucking amazing, just like John Walks Long. My chest tightens. I wanted to make him the head of the Crossroads so he could rule with wisdom and compassion. My second choice would've been Brother Ash, but fate didn't give me any choice but Jeremiah, the one guy who actually manages to out-macho Tony.

"What about the other Crossroads clans? Who do they support?"

"Clans allied with the Beggars will support you. The Shinobi will support our uncle because of their enmity with Jeremiah. The rest could go either way."

"What about our clan? Are they loyal to us or Uncle George?" Notice I said us instead of me? I'm sure Tony did, but he won't show it.

"Kowloon supports you. Wanchai is siding with our uncle."

I expected that. Wanchai is in the hands of the Chans, the family that controls the wealth of our clan. My grandfather, Damian, was hitched to one of their daughters, Tiffany, in an arranged marriage. Pretty typical in our clan and most people suck that up, but not him. As soon as Tiffany gave birth to twin boys, Gramps ran off with a woman he made his Second Wife. I don't know much about it. They all died before I was born, but the bitterness lingers because my dad supported his father instead of his mother. I've never been to the Wanchai *kongsi* and barely know my grandmother's family. It was different for Tony and Aaron since Uncle George supported Tiffany and was always more of a Chan than a Lau.

"So, now that the truth is out, they cut you off?" I ask.

Tony nods once.

I rub my forehead. All this shit that has nothing to do with us is now biting us in the ass. Bad blood is spilling into the next generation and all we can do is deal with it. "So, Uncle George has the clan compound and the financial backing of the Chans?"

"Yes, but that's the only support he has. Worldwide, more than half the *kongsis* have declared their support for you. The rest refuse to commit. That will change in favor of whoever finds the Yang Pearl." He shakes his head. "I can't believe it's lost. Our father must have hidden it someplace safe, but where?"

"Yeah, about that…" My heart starts pounding. For the past two years, I've wanted to prove to Tony that his mother murdered mine. Now, justice is at hand and it's twisting my stomach into knots. What if I'm wrong? No. I know I'm right, but… damn. I'm not opening old wounds. I'm stabbing a knife into fresh ones.

"What?"

"Remember, after my mother died, I told you I saw Auntie Sylvia with her hands around Mom's neck." If I'd said this before yesterday, Tony would've stopped me right here. Now, he's silent, listening. "Both Head Elder and Uncle George said the Yang Pearl wasn't on Dad when he died. I think he must have given it to Mom for safekeeping and that Auntie Sylvia took it from her after she… after she did what she did."

Tony shakes his head. "If that's true, I would have found it after she died."

"Did you check all her stuff, like, I dunno, her jewelry box?"

He freezes. He doesn't blink, but I can almost see the gears turning in his head. Then he sucks in a slow breath. "Before Mother died, she told me she was leaving all her jewelry to me. I had to promise no one else would take the box or even open it. I thought she was trying to keep my father… uncle from taking it. After she died, I gave the box to May, but she didn't want it. Mother didn't like her and May said she wouldn't feel right wearing her jewelry. She suggested we put the box away and perhaps give what's inside as wedding gifts to our children."

May is a nice person. I'm sure what she meant was, 'Your mother was a mega-bitch and treated me like shit, and I wouldn't be caught dead wearing her crap. Let's pretend we're going to give it to our kids so I don't have to look at that box for another twenty years.'

"So, you never opened it?"

His hands clench into fists. He gets up and strides out of the room.

My nerves jangle and I start pacing. This is it. Really it. I almost want to cry. I slow to a stop at the mantle and stare at the framed photos, mostly of Tony and May's wedding. It was a small affair, considering his mother's illness and his father's… former father's absence. Auntie Cat flew down with Uncle Roy to attend the banquet, but I refused to go. There's a photo of Tony and Aaron standing together in their tuxes and I feel my absence. I shouldn't have been such a dick. I should have been here for him. At the end of the mantle, though, there is a photo of the three of us, taken years ago by Dad at the beach. We stand in birth order, Aaron and I grinning while Tony looks solemn and responsible, even while on vacation.

From as far back as I can remember, Tony went with us everywhere. I always thought it was because Uncle George was a lousy father. The truth had been there all along and none of us saw it.

Tony comes back in, lugging the largest jewelry box I've ever seen. I roll my eyes. Auntie Sylvia didn't work and had no interest in martial arts or any kind of clan activities except high profile banquets. She spent her time shopping, having her hair and nails done, and going to lunch with her snooty frenemies. She and Mom wouldn't have been friends even if Dad hadn't come between them.

He sets the box on the coffee table and uses a key to open the lock. I suck in my breath as he opens the lid. The thick, oily stench of roses wafts out and gags me. There, on top of a glittering hoard of diamonds and pearls, are a black pouch and a sealed envelope. Tony reaches for the pouch and pulls open the string. The Yang Pearl tumbles into his hand, its thick gold chain coiling around his fingers.

His gasp of pain makes my chest hurt.

He hands me the pearl before sinking into his chair. Warmth spreads through my palm as I feel the familiar thrum of energy. I look at him and nod. "This is it."

He shakes his head and mumbles. "She did it. She really did it." Then he leans forward and snatches the envelope. He rips it open and leans back as he reads the sheets of paper inside.

I barely breathe. I close my hand around the Yang Pearl. Its energy flows through me like a low-key electric charge. I want to place it around my neck and feel that surge of dragon power, but I can't. Not if I want Tony to accept being the Dragon Son.

Tony covers his face as he crushes the letter in his fist. At first, I don't think he's going to let me read it. Then he tosses it on the table, gets up, and leaves the room.

I smooth out the pages, take a deep breath, and read.

Lennon

Son,

After you read this, you will hate me. I am glad I will not live to see that hatred in your eyes.

I roll my eyes. What a fucking drama queen to the bitter end. I scan the page, looking at her jagged handwriting. Was she angry or scared, or both? Also, it pisses me off that she wrote in English instead of Chinese. She liked to brag that because she went to boarding school in England, her English is far superior to someone who went to school in Hong Kong. That someone was my mother, whose English was perfectly good, just not snooty and pretentious.

Even in her confession, she has to take a final dig at Mom. Why am I reading this self-pitying poison? I crumple the pages, ready to throw it in the fireplace and strike a match. Then I stop because the paper is sticking to my hands like glue. However much I hate her, I need read her admission of guilt. It has to be here. Why else would Tony react that way? I straighten the pages and continue reading.

Please understand that everything I did was to ensure your birthright, from the beginning before I even conceived you. Yes, you were robbed of your rightful place even then. How can that be? I will explain.

When I was ten years old, I was betrothed to Michael Lau, the Dragon Son's Heir. His brother, George, was betrothed to Michelle, the only daughter of Head Elder. I was raised to be the Dragon Son's wife. I was already the granddaughter of Third Elder and felt secure in my destiny to give birth to and nurture the next heir.

Everything changed when Jade Dragon's comet appeared. Head Elder became obsessed with that comet. He believed it heralded the birth of the next dragon and he wanted that dragon to be his grandson.

I found all that out yesterday, when Head Elder finally realized I'm not the next dragon and never will be, thanks to my dad. At least, that's who he blames. All this hatred and misery over a half-baked prophesy that'll never come true. How can a human become a dragon?

My grandfather had just died, and my father was determined to succeed him. Head Elder agreed to make him Third Elder in exchange for annulling my betrothal to Michael and giving me instead to George. My father exchanged my happiness and purpose in life for his greed and desire for power. Words cannot describe how much I hated him for this, him and my mother both.

My only weapon was defiance. It served me badly. My parents punished and threatened me until I agreed to marry George. In my heart, I knew my true husband was Michael. I had to make him my ally. I tried convincing him we were meant to be together, but he didn't care. He didn't think there was much difference between marrying me or Michelle and would do his duty, regardless. He was young, so I forgave him. I didn't give up.

Head Elder wanted Michelle's marriage to Michael timed so he could have his dragon grandson. Ordinarily, a younger brother wouldn't marry before the eldest, but Michael and George were twins, so it was decided that George and I would be married first. I had run out of time and needed to win Michael over to my side. The only way to do that was to lure him into my bed. It wasn't hard to get him to betray his brother. I confessed my feelings and shed a few tears over my fate. He brought me a rose and I gave him a shy kiss, and didn't stop him when he wanted more.

I shudder and skim over the details of their hookups. Why is she telling Tony all this? It's gross, and inappropriate, and one big pity party.

I thought I had him, but there was one problem. He insisted on using condoms. Your father wasn't a fool. He knew I wanted him to impregnate me and he used my desperation in trade for sex as if I were a whore.

Ugh! I want to bleach my eyes. Why was Dad being such a dick?

Michael gloated and smirked whenever he saw me with George. He'd had me first. I was a notch in his belt, a conquest in the war between brothers, to be used and discarded at will. He didn't realize I was using him, poking needles in the condoms when he wasn't looking.

The night before my wedding, I told him what I'd done, and that I was pregnant. I said he was marrying me and that was final. If not, I'd tell Head Elder everything.

He called me a stupid cunt. He said Head Elder would call off my marriage to George. Then, I'd be forced to have an abortion and be banished from the clan. No one would believe my story because I'd be accused of dallying with an outsider and trying to save face by claiming the Dragon Son had dishonored me. My family would disown me. I would have no friends, no money, no support.

This is how he spoke to me, the mother of his child, the mother of the next Dragon Son, the girl who loved him. I should have hated him, but I couldn't. I needed to play a new game. All he said would happen and I couldn't take that risk. Scared and alone, I agreed to marry his brother without another word of protest.

I couldn't stand being touched by George, but I endured, playing the sweet young wife and wheedling him into staying in the San

Francisco kongsi, much as I despised it and the filthy slum that surrounds it. I was determined to remain and give birth to you here, and force Michael to watch his son grow and thrive. Then, right before Michael was to marry Michelle, I struck again. I told George that his brother was the father of my son.

Michael denied it. There was a paternity test, and the truth came out. I expected George to leave me. By this time, I thought Michael would love his son enough to claim him, and me, as his own.

I was wrong. George couldn't care less about my fidelity. It wasn't in his best interest to alienate my family or cause them to lose face because of my actions. Michael refused to acknowledge you and threatened us both with shame and expulsion. The brothers worked things out between them and George was well-pleased having Michael forever in his debt.

All I could do was hate. I hated Michael and his sick, useless wife that could bear only one weak child. I hated my husband and parents. There are few people I don't hate. Perhaps only my sons. I wish I could lie and claim Aaron as Michael's child, but I'm at the end of my life and I must admit, Michael never touched me again, no matter how available I made myself to him. George wanted a child of his own and I capitulated. I first became pregnant with a girl, but I aborted her and claimed it was a miscarriage. Sons give a woman power. Their fathers gave me anything I asked. I could go anywhere and buy anything. All I lacked was love and a sense of belonging.

I stop reading because I want to puke. I swallow hard against the burning in my throat. Dad and Uncle George were both such bastards, and Auntie Sylvia… had she ever done anything, one single thing in her entire life that wasn't out of self-interest? Even her supposed love for Tony is all about her becoming queen.

Years passed and there was little I could do except make sure your father saw you often. I raised you to be righteous and brave, intelligent, a matchless warrior, and a son any man would be proud to claim, one that shined bright compared to his pathetic second son.

Guilt and remorse ate away at him as he watched you grow and thrive. He loved you and wanted to claim you. Before he left for Hong Kong, he told me he would admit it all, to Michelle and Head Elder. He would right his wrongs and make my son his heir.

In my heart, I felt boundless joy, but I contained my outward appearance. No one could suspect, not until I took my rightful place as mother of the future Dragon Son. I knew there would be shame and disapproval, but I didn't care. Regardless of what anyone said, they couldn't deny my son was first born and the true heir. That's what I believed, and once again, I was wrong.

Head Elder would have none of it. Paul was born in the year of the comet. He was the new dragon and the next Dragon Son. He threatened you and me with death if the truth came out. So, Michael made the biggest mistake of his life. He turned to his brother. I don't know what he offered or promised, but George agreed to help him against Head Elder.

Shit. I rub my forehead. No way. How could Dad be so stupid? Or was he that desperate?

George went straight to Head Elder and offered to betray Michael. Head Elder agreed and they set their plan in motion to deny my son his rightful place. Michael met with George in Kowloon and Shinobi waylaid them. Instead of fighting with Michael, they showed him a live video of you. They told Michael that either he or you would die, right then. His choice.

Your father died to save you. Always remember that. I can almost forgive him everything because of this.

How do I know all this? George told me this story to torment my dying days. Instead, it gave me hope. But I get ahead of myself.

When I learned your father died, I went mad with grief. I'd lost the love of my life. My son would never be the Dragon Son. I could not - would not accept this. I went to Michelle's room to confront her and found her collapsed on the bed like the weakling she was. I knew about her heart condition and that I should call a doctor, but I wanted her to suffer and die. Then I saw it around her neck. She was wearing the Yang Pearl. Michael must have given it to her when she left Hong Kong.

I tried to take it, but her eyes opened. She knew what I was doing. She'd tell Head Elder and see me dead or disgraced. I had to act. I grabbed the pillow and smothered her. Then I took the Yang Pearl.

I close my eyes and shudder as anger runs through me, hot and cold. It's strange how, even though I knew she was guilty, I needed her to confess. I won't ever get closure, but at least there's no longer any shadow of doubt hanging over her guilt.

A secret autopsy was performed, showing Chelle had been smothered, just as Paul said. Head Elder wanted me punished without alienating my family. He contacted the Five Venom Clan. They gave him a slow-acting poison that mimics pancreatic cancer. Even doctors can't tell the difference. Once ingested, there is no cure. I was forced to endure chemotherapy and radiation, knowing they were useless. I suffer. I cannot tell you how this pain eats me from the inside. You need to know the truth, so I write this letter while I still can. I must finish it now before the pain makes it impossible.

Whatever punishment you think fits my crimes, know I suffered greatly while I lived.

My only source of happiness in life was you.

Take the Yang Pearl. Be the Dragon Son. It is your right.

Lennon

Damn. Evil. Murdering.

"Bitch." I spit the word out. It isn't enough. No words are enough to describe Auntie Sylvia. All those lives ruined, all because she wanted to be the mother of the Dragon Son. I'm glad she suffered. I wish she was still alive and could suffer more. Worst of all, I didn't get revenge. Head Elder did. Auntie Sylvia will never be convicted for her crimes. Her only punishment was pain and knowing her sons would hate her.

Her sons. I hear their angry voices coming from the hall. I jump off the ottoman and run out there.

Tony and Aaron are standing at the alcove where Auntie Sylvia's altar used to be. I say 'used to' because Tony has torn it down and shoved everything into a trash can, including her spirit tablet. Chinese people believe a spirit tablet contains part of the soul of a dead person. That's why we venerate them and place offerings. We believe our ancestors are still with us through these tablets, so, tossing your mother's tablet in the trash is one of the worst things you can do.

"No! Give it to me!" Aaron shouts. He shoves his brother. Tony doesn't budge. Aaron shoves again and tries reaching around him to grab the can. Tony pushes him against the wall. Aaron pants, his face red with anguish. Then he launches off the wall for another attack.

"Aaron," I call out. He stops. I turn to Tony. "Big Brother, I know you're angry."

"I am beyond anger." Tony speaks with a frozen fire in his eyes.

"Okay. I'm sure you know how I feel, too, but don't do something you'll regret."

He jerks his head at Aaron. "Show him the letter."

I start to say no. I don't want to. He's just a kid, the same age I was when my parents were murdered. Then I sigh. I was a kid who wanted the truth and no one would give it to me. How can I deny Aaron, no matter how hard it is on him?

"What letter?" asks Aaron, his eyes wary. "Doesn't matter. I'm not going anywhere until you give me Mother's tablet."

"Tony won't do anything until you read it, right?" I look at Tony like, come on, man, be reasonable.

His chest rises and fall. Then he nods once.

I tug Aaron's arm. "Come on." He doesn't move, so I tug harder until I'm dragging him down the hall. When we get to the living room, the first thing I show Aaron is the Yang Pearl.

His mouth gapes open. "Wait. Is that…?"

"Yeah."

"But, where…" He looks at his mother's jewelry box. He sinks the couch, his voice lowering to a bare whisper. "She had it?"

"Yeah." I hand him the letter. I don't want to watch him read it. Watching Tony was hard enough. I leave the room, but I stop halfway down the hall.

May is standing beside Tony, her hand on his arm, and her face soft and sympathetic, but also firm. She's got this old soul wisdom about her that I like and Tony desperately needs.

His voice rises. "I don't want it in the building. I don't want it anywhere near me."

She also speaks louder but remains calm. "I'll send it to her family's shrine in Wanchai."

"I want it gone now."

"Then I'll do it now."

He doesn't resist as she reaches around him and takes the spirit tablet out of the can. Then she walks away, toward the stairs. He picks up the can and follows her down.

I go back to the living room to tell Aaron so he won't flip his shit. He looks up from the letter, unshed tears sparkling in his eyes. "Tell Tony to throw it away." Then he drops the letter and shoulders past me to leave the room.

I finally understand what people mean when they say they're filled with emptiness. My family finally believes me. I'm not a crazy person accusing an innocent woman of murder. I guess I pictured it different. That they would learn the truth and apologize for doubting me. Instead, they're shattered, the way I was on that awful day.

Part of me wants to set the letter on fire and watch it burn, the way I hope Auntie Sylvia is burning in hell. Another part of me wants to put the letter in my pocket and take it somewhere to seal away as evidence. Do I want expose her crimes to the entire Crossroads? Yes. Do I want Tony and Aaron to suffer the consequences? No. There's also a shitty side of me that sees this as another obstacle. Auntie Sylvia's karma was as bad as her actions. Everything she strived for turned against her, exactly like she deserved, but now it's biting me in the ass. How will I convince Tony to be the Dragon Son now?

I can't take or destroy the letter, so I do the next best thing and take photos of each page. I might want to read it again. Or I might want to print the photos and set them on fire. Who knows? I can barely think straight.

May enters the living room, her face pale and weary from

bearing the burden of an unborn child along with her husband's suffering. She catches me taking a photo of the last page. Our eyes meet. I don't know what to say, so I say nothing. Her lips thin before she sighs as if deciding this isn't her battle. She's a doctor and someone who prefers a quiet, family-oriented life. Being the Dragon Son's Wife is the last thing she wants, which makes me feel shitty for wanting to thrust it on her.

She speaks softly. "Your Big Brother is in his office. He's locked the door and doesn't want to see anyone. I don't know how long he'll be in there. Please stay. You can rest in the guest room. The bed is made."

"Thanks, but I can't. I gotta go. Sorry."

"You should stay. He needs you."

Shit. I know that, but Penny needs me, too. Will I always feel torn between them? I shake my head. "I'm sorry, but I need to be alone. When Tony's ready, ask him to call me, okay?"

She nods, just once, mimicking her husband's style almost perfectly, before leaving the room.

I pick up the pendant and dangle it so it sways; the pearl catching the light. Jade Dragon's power vibrates through the heavy gold chain and into my fingers. What would happen if I leave the Yang Pearl here? Will Tony wear it and accept his fate as Dragon Son? Fat chance. I can't just leave it in the living room unguarded and there's no one else to trust it with except me. With a long sigh, I place it around my neck.

Warmth spreads through my chest as it activates my *chi*. My entire body tingles as dragon energy races through my limbs. Whoa. What a rush. I close my eyes and wait for the energy to disperse and subside. I sense Jade Dragon frolicking with a pod of whales near the Channel Islands. He knows I'm wearing the Yang Pearl. He's too far away for us to communicate and I don't want to talk to him, anyway.

All the doors in the hallway are closed as I leave. Despite her photo being trashed, I can still feel Auntie Sylvia's diamond eyes follow me as I head downstairs.

While on the bus, I check my texts. Most of them are from Auntie Cat, a string of sad messages from a lonely woman put in an impossible position by her shitty brothers. I'm still not ready to talk to her, but my first stop is her house to pick up my scooter. It's parked in front of her building and I can feel her looking out at me from the bay window on the second floor. My phone buzzes. It's her.

Are you coming home?

This has never been my home, but that's not her fault. I don't look up, but I do text back.

I'm picking up my scooter. I can't talk yet.
Maybe tomorrow.

Are you all right?

No. You?

No. There are things I need to tell you.

There are things I need to tell her, too. Should I wait for Tony's permission? No. To get the whole truth out of Auntie Cat, I'll need her to read Auntie Sylvia's letter. I text her the photos.

This letter was in Auntie Sylvia's jewelry box
along with the Yang Pearl. Read it and we'll
talk about it tomorrow. Don't tell anyone
but Roy.

I shove my phone in my pocket in a very obvious way so she'll see I'm done. Then I get on my scooter and head for the bank. The teller is sympathetic to my tale of stolen cards and promises to send immediate replacements. As I leave, my phone buzzes. I want to ignore it. I don't want to talk or even text with anyone in my family right now, but what if it's… I check my screen and exhale at the sight of Penny's name.

Hey, I got my phone back.

I talked to Tony. It didn't go so good.

Kai told me. He heard from Aaron. I'm so sorry. Are you ok?

No. I'm going to my studio.

It's weird, because I want to be alone, but I want to be alone with her.

Do you want to come with me? I have my scooter so I can pick you up.

Ok. I'll meet you outside.

The tightness in my chest loosens enough for me to take an easy breath. As long as I have Penny, I know I can face all this.

Penny

Bridie pours whiskey into her tea and takes a grim sip. "I don't know how much more I can take. Don't they realize the torture we're going through? How important this is?"

Kai and I exchange looks. Doesn't she realize what Lennon's family is going through? Maybe she can't. Maybe all she can think about is Matthew and nothing else matters. I want Matthew back, too, more than anything, but fact is, we need Tony and he's just been dealt a bitter blow.

"Aaron says Tony's not talking to anyone. I mean, can you blame him?" asks Kai.

She takes another sip and mutters, "I blame anyone who comes between me and your father."

What is it about Bridie that she can't face life without a crutch? During her short, disastrous marriage to Bill, she kept a bottle hidden under the sink and would pour herself "a wee dram" when he wasn't looking. I tried to pretend it wasn't a big deal, that I didn't notice the deeper her sadness, the more she would tipple. After we untangled ourselves from Bill and Kingfisher, Bridie seemed to stop drinking aside from a pint at the pub after our shows. Has she been tippling all this time, easing the pain of missing Gerry and Matthew? If so, only Matty's return will make her give it up because she'll have him to lean on again.

I motion with my head. Kai follows me out of the kitchen and into my bedroom where I sit on the floor and reach for my Doc Martens. His eyes widen. "You going somewhere?"

"Lennon is coming to pick me up."

"Don't leave me alone with her."

"Sorry, but I have to. We need to figure out what we're going to do next."

"Can't you do that here?"

I look up from the lacing my boots. "What do you think Bridie will do the moment he walks through the door?"

"Jump down his throat?"

"And then?"

"Wail like a banshee?"

"Exactly." I reach into my stash of scarves and pull out the first one I grab hold of, a shimmery, beaded confection that looks odd with my distressed leggings and funky chunky jumper. I knot it around my neck and sling my boho bag across my shoulder. A quick glance in the mirror shows a hot mess I can't be bothered to fix.

Kai grimaces, but it's not from my choice of duds. "How long will you be gone?"

"Dunno. We'll be at his studio."

"Yeah?"

"Yeah."

He cocks his head and raises his eyebrows.

My hands go to my hips. "We'll be talking, not shagging, if that's what you're asking."

"Argh!" He covers his ears. "But, don't you have to do… that so you and Lennon can use the pearls together?"

"Not anymore. Tony's the Dragon Son. He's the first-born

and that's how their…" I wave a hand, searching for words, "magic works."

"Yeah." He stretches the word out.

"Did Aaron tell you something different?"

Kai reaches for his phone and scrolls until he gets to the right message. He holds the screen out to me.

> There's no way Tony will be Dragon Son now.
> He said Mother's sin has tainted his blood.

Air hisses through my teeth. "Like I said, Lennon and I need to talk."

As we pass the kitchen, Bridie looks up, her eyes darting between my boots and purse. She drops her shaking head and reaches for the bottle. It's like she's tugging on a cord of guilt that's wrapped around my heart. I have to keep moving or I won't be able to leave.

When we get to the front door, I whisper, "Look after Mum."

He breathes out an "Okay." I can feel his forlorn gaze follow me down the hall.

When I get outside, my heartbeat quickens at the sight of Lennon, even though I saw him a few hours ago. He's taken off his helmet and is wearing those round John Lennon glasses that made him the Owl Boy I fell in love with.

Yeah, okay, I am in love with him. Not that it's anyone's business.

"Hey," he says without a smile. Not that he has much to smile about right now.

"Hey. You okay?"

He shakes his head.

My family needs his family to solve all their problems, pronto, but it ain't gonna happen. I put on my helmet and climb on behind him. As my arms go around his waist I get that feeling, like I always do, that we fit perfectly together, like our bodies were made for each other. Does he feel the same way? I feel his chest rise and fall. Then he reaches for my hand and squeezes.

"Thanks," he says.

"For what?"

"For coming with me after everything that's happened."

"That's what friends do."

A smile cocks his lips so it's almost a smirk as he says, "Then, thanks, friend."

Friends first. That's what we are and what I have to remember as my heart pounds against his back while we drive through the city. The air gets colder as we approach the bay and drive along its shore, and I snuggle closer to Lennon for warmth. The last shower he took was in my bathroom and he smells like my soap. That shouldn't feel sexy, except it does and I'm glad for the wind that cools my cheeks.

Lennon's studio is part of an artists' collective in a warehouse on Pier 36. We park outside and get off the scooter, and stand there in this weird awkwardness, like we're both afraid to go inside but don't want to say so. Then we speak at the same time.

"Are you hungry?"

"Have you had lunch?"

That nudges awkward laughs out of both of us. Lennon scratches the back of his head. "*Banh mi?*"

My mouth waters. "Hell, yeah."

There's no stoplight nearby, so we wait for traffic to clear before we run across the Embarcadero, being careful not to trip over the light rail tracks running down the middle of the road. When we reach the sidewalk, Lennon holds out his hand and I take it. As our palms touch, a zing of energy runs up my arm and spreads across my chest. I jump and he grasps my hand harder as if he thinks I'm going to fall.

"Are you okay?" he asks.

"Yeah…" I wiggle my hand in his. No joy buzzer and why would he do that, anyway? It must've been static electricity. "Let's go."

We walk several blocks, threading our way through the lunch crowd churning in and out of the office buildings, until we reach Banh Jovi, a tiny Vietnamese sandwich shop. We join the line outside and stand close together, our arms and shoulders touching. I still feel it, some kind of low key electric current emanating from him. Maybe it's my imagination, but it feels more real than that. We both order lemongrass tofu sandwiches and *cafe su da*, sweet iced coffee, and I pay because even though Lennon has more money than me, I don't like feeling dependent on anyone.

"I'll pay next time," he says as we walk away.

I shrug because as long as things are equitable, it's all good. Seeing Bridie so dependent on men has done things to me. Maybe that's why I can't just fall into Lennon's arms no matter how I feel.

After another dash across the Embarcadero, we enter the Kinetic Collective. Most of the occupants are full-time artists, so the place is always bustling with activity. At the far end of the warehouse, Junkyard Metallurgy is putting the final touches on Doris, their giant spider. Some of them are dressed all in black, including facial mesh, as if to appear invisible while working the mechanisms that make Doris move up and down her web.

"Cool," I say as we head up the winding staircase.

"They're looking for volunteers," quips Lennon. "Includes free entrance to Monstrosity."

"What's Monstrosity?"

"Some big Halloween thing happening at Civic Auditorium."

"Pass. We usually spend Halloween at whatever Nest we're

near. Everyone puts on fancy dress and there's a big party, and the Upright Man lights a huge bonfire."

"Halloween's big with Strowlers?"

"Well, yeah. The Irish sort of invented it."

He smirks. "No way."

"Yeah, way. Before Christianity, November 1 was our New Year's Day, except we called it Samhain. We believe that on New Year's Eve, ghosts and fairies openly walk among the living and can even take you into their realms. We appease the spirits with gifts or frighten them off with fire. Anyway, the Church didn't like that kind of fun, so they changed it. swapping fairies and ghosts with saints and demons and called it All Hallows Eve. Get it? Hallows E'en. Halloween."

"Oh wow. Yeah. For real, huh?"

"For real. Strowlers still consider Samhain to be New Year's Day. To us, it's the beginning of winter and a mass migration, either into Nests or south, into warmer countries like France and Spain."

"We do something kind of similar. I mean, the Two Dragon Clan. There's this thing called the Ghost Festival and basically the entire of August is Ghost Month. We're supposed to venerate our ancestors and appease the ghosts with no one left to worship them. The fifteenth day of that month is Ghost Day, but the actual dates shift around because it's measured by the Lunar Calendar."

"Sorta like Easter?"

"Sorta. Anyway, Jade Dragon died in his human form the day before Ghost Day, so it's become a big event in our clan. We call it the Summoning Ceremony and it's when Jade Dragon comes to our ancestral hall and speaks to the Dragon Son."

We stop in front of his studio door and my arms fold. "Wait. So, you're saying the dragon talks to the Dragon Son? I mean, like, actually speaks to him?"

"Yeah, I guess." He pivots away to open the door. I bite my lip. I hope he doesn't think I was taking the piss. Jade Dragon seems to be sort of like religion to them and I wouldn't make fun of that. I'm just curious.

I wait outside the studio while he uses his phone to scan for hidden cameras and microphones. He nods the all clear and I enter. The leggings I'd spray painted to sell in my online store are still hanging where I left them and the splattered stencils he used for his latest graffiti are still spread across his work table. It's like our former lives have been waiting for us to return. I want to return. I liked that life.

Lennon turns on the overhead fan and its white noise soothes my nerves. We settle cross-legged on the bed and I wrap a blanket around me like I always do. It smells like us even though all we've ever done is kiss. My bed must smell the same. The thought makes me feel things and I take a big bite of my sandwich so I'll feel something else. Pro tip: lemongrass tofu and *cafe su da* are a sweet and spicy flavor, almost as good as kisses. We don't talk much because anything we have to say will kill our appetites.

After we're done, we lay back and stare at the steel-beamed ceiling. It's so comfortable that part of me wants to fall asleep. Another part of me wants to roll over for some sweet and spicy kisses. Instead, I squeeze Lennon's hand and that tingling feeling races through me again. I snatch away my hand and roll up onto my elbow.

"What is that?"

He rolls up to face me. "You feel something?"

"Don't you?"

"Yeah," he breathes out. "It must be the Yang Pearl."

"You're wearing it?"

"Yeah."

"Can I see it?"

He tugs on a gold chain under his shirt and pulls out an

amulet with a large, luminous pearl at its center. I reach out and, since he doesn't draw away, I touch it. A strong hum of energy tingles through my body and I gasp. "Wow. Was that you?"

"Maybe? I'm still figuring out how to use it."

"Are you supposed to use it? I mean, if Tony's the Dragon Son. Is he? Or," I take a hard breath, "are you?"

He looks down as if he doesn't want me reading his expression. "It's hard to explain. I wish we could use the Silent Speech."

"What's that?"

"What it sounds like, talking without speaking."

"Can you teach me?"

"Yeah." He lifts his gaze and rubs his chin. "Actually, the Yang Pearl will make it easier for us to connect. Thing is, Silent Speech is super personal. You have to trust the other person completely because our minds touch. And it creates this bond that doesn't go away, even when that trust is broken."

"Sounds like you're speaking from experience."

"Yeah. Me and Tony. Me and Auntie Cat."

"Maybe because you've never stopped trusting them?"

"Yeah, maybe. Anyway, we'll have that same bond. I mean, for life."

Like what I feel for him will ever go away. "Don't we already?"

His chest rises and falls as a wistful intensity fills his eyes. "How I feel about you, it's kind of all mixed up because of… you know, stuff. Except that I know we'll always be friends."

"Exactly. So, let's do the thing."

We lay down and Lennon clasps my hand. He turns his head and I can feel his breath soft in my ear. "I'm going to transfer some of my *chi* to you. Then you transfer some of yours to me. After that, I'll touch your mind and you let me in."

I close my eyes and feel warmth transfer from his hand to mine, spreading up my arm in a soft tingle. I go with that flow, emptying my mind in favor of sensation because Lennon had warned me that over-thinking *chi* always messes up the soft arts. You have to let go to let it happen. So I do, focusing on my *chi* as if it's a stream in the forest, flowing through me and into him. Our energy mingles, becoming strength and weakness as it flows in and out of each of us. Then something joins our flow; the energy from the Yang Pearl. It threads through and unites us to it and each other. The canvas mattress seems wavy, like we're floating on the surface of the ocean. Something huge and reptilian swims beneath us, but we're not afraid. It's just a dragon. I feel a light tap on my consciousness. I direct my flow of *chi* there and the feeling becomes stronger as if someone were knocking on a door, and through it I can hear a soft voice.

Penny?

I open the door.

Lennon?

Yeah. Hi.

Hi? Is that all you can say? We're talking with our minds.

I know. I've done it before.

How long can we keep this up?

As long as we want. It drains our chi, but not to the degree of most skills.

Is the pearl doing something?

You felt that?

Yeah, like it was us and something else. I expect him to say it was his dragon, but he doesn't. *Do we have to be in physical contact to do this?* He shakes his head. I don't let go. *What happened when you saw Tony?*

He tells me and he's right. It's easier to understand this way because I can feel his emotions, his rage and elation, as he reads Sylvia's confession. Then I feel his sorrow as he watches Aaron cry and Tony lose control. It's beyond the sense of sympathy when someone shares a terrible story. I'm drained when he finishes and have to speak aloud. "Will Tony change his mind?"

"He has to. Healing Matthew won't matter much to him, but getting back the Yin Pearl is huge. He won't want Uncle George getting to it before us."

My phone buzzes and I squint at the garble on my screen from Bridie.

> TONY LAU WHY WONT HE DRAGON
> SON??? IMPORTANT!!! DOES HE KNOW I I
> GO TALK HIM

> No! Mum, wait. I'll be home soon.

> R U W LENNON??!@

> Mum, turn off the caps lock and settle down.

My phone pings with a message from Kai.

> She's drunk. Come home now.

Another ping. Bridie's next text is pure gibberish. I look up from the screen. "Bridie's going mental. I need to go home."

"I'll give you a ride."

Ordinarily, I take the bus home since he basically lives here, but these aren't ordinary times. George could try kidnapping me again if I'm on my own. Still, I hesitate because I don't like depending on him or anyone. Then I feel it - that touch on my consciousness like a brush against my soul. I open up. I sense Lennon's emotion with each word.

Let me give you a ride, okay? So I know you got home safe.

My heart beats faster. I want to respond by kissing him, but if I do, we'll keep kissing and that's a bad idea. Instead, I pour my own feelings into my response. *I can't live in fear for the rest of my life. I'll do whatever it takes to save Matthew and my family. And you. You won't be safe until we stop your uncle and we can only do that with both pearls.*

Same. Whatever it takes. Our chests rise and fall together. *This is kind of intense, huh?*

Is it always like this?

No. Not with my family. This is the first time I made the connection with a friend.

And we're more than friends. *Meet back here tomorrow morning?*

Yeah. Or maybe you can come back here tonight?

Maybe. We stare into each other's eyes, but before our lips can touch, our phones buzz simultaneously. We stare at our screens.

ILL DIE I I CANT BEE WIT MATTY AGN

I groan through my gritted teeth. "No, not tonight."

Lennon looks up from his phone. "Tony wants to see me in the morning."

And there it is. The needs of our families have always come between us. And maybe always will.

Today, I feel more like a delivery boy than a boss as I ride up to the *kongsi* on my Vespa. Maybe I should swap it for a badass Ducati like the one Tony has. As if that will do the trick. Nothing will make me feel like the Dragon Son, especially here, the scene of so many crimes. I couldn't stop Mom's murder. Dad couldn't stop himself from being a dick. Auntie Sylvia made everyone pay for her misery. How can I ever live here again, let alone rule the clan? Tony's got the… what's that phrase again? Intestinal fortitude. When I learned it in AP English, I immediately thought of him. Someone with courage and endurance that comes from the gut. Anyway, he's got what it takes to live here and be the boss. I just need to convince him he deserves it and that's gonna be hard because that's where his intestinal fortitude reaches its limit.

As I get off my scooter, five men enter the alley, striding toward me in a V-shaped attack formation. The guy in front looks familiar and as they get closer, I realize he's Brother Seven of the Eagle Beaks, one of the smaller Chinatown clans. Not gangsters, but on the fringes, like they go that way when it suits their purposes. He reminds me of Jeremiah Walks Long.

Same swagger and perma-scowl, except Jeremiah has cred from being a combat veteran. I don't know shit about this guy.

He comes to a stop half-way down the alley and hollers, "Dragon Son, I challenge you. Here and now."

I should've seen this coming, since punking out of my fight with Jeremiah has put a target on my back. Our clan is still the head Crossroads clan in Chinatown, which means every chief with a hard-on to rule is going to challenge me.

Since I don't have time for this bullshit, I holler back, "Fuck off."

He gets this Scooby Doo 'ruh-roh!' look, like he can't believe what he heard. He slows to a stop and cross his arms as his dude-bros surround him. "Coward. The Two Dragon Clan is done. We're taking over Chinatown."

Okay, now he's pissing me off. Usually, anger is bad for my *chi*, but I feel it triggering something within the depths of the Yang Pearl. A surge of adrenaline rushes through my body, pumping up my muscles and amplifying my strength. Dude thinks he can beat me? No one can beat me. Not him. Not Jeremiah. I could kick their asses at the same time without breaking a sweat.

I gesture with both hands. "Come at me, bro."

Brother Seven does a Scooby head shake before rolling his shoulders, lifting his fists and charging forward.

I grin while dodging the clumsy punches he throws. My roundhouse kick connects with his ribs and sends him reeling. He clutches his side, wheezing, his nostrils flared, and eyes narrowed with frustration. What a loser. I can read his moves before he makes them. My smirk makes him rage-snort, and he comes at me again, punching and kicking while I bob and duck, still grinning. Then he spins out of a sweep kick and as he comes up, my knee connects with his chin. Blood spurts from his mouth as he tumbles back, falling hard on the pavement. He lay there for a few moments before rolling over, his jaw hanging open as guttural howls emit from his clogged throat. He scuttles back toward his men, who surround him as I sneer at them. Who's the coward now?

Him or me?

My adrenaline evaporates. I'm an eighteen-year-old kid who doesn't have that kind of muscle power, not naturally. Not without the Yang Pearl. Holy shit. Is this why the Dragon Sons are undefeated? Crossroads challenges forbid *chi* abilities, but wearing a protective amulet is standard practice. No one would know the Dragon Son was getting a boost of dragon power. Which means the Two Dragon Clan has been cheating all along.

No wonder Head Elder and Uncle George were grilling me about the Yang Pearl. Without it, Uncle George doesn't have a chance in hell of winning any challenges. He's a scholar, not a warrior, and the only martial abilities he excels at are the stealth skills.

That means when they find out about this fight, they'll know I have the Yang Pearl.

Shit.

I turn toward the *kongsi* and see Tony and some guards standing out front, watching me act like the legit Dragon Son. Well, shit. Not good. As I join them, the guards step aside, heads inclined, before one rushes to hold the door open. Damn it!

Tony and I don't speak until we're inside and he gives his single manly nod. "You handled that well, but no more profanity. It cheapens your position as head of our clan."

Shit, shit, shit.

I follow him upstairs, my head spinning with how to spin this in another direction. We pass the nook in the hallway, now scrubbed clean of Auntie Sylvia. Even the rose stench has disappeared, replaced by a strong pine scent. When we get to the living room, I glance at the mantlepiece. Her photos have all been removed, along with those of Dad and Uncle George. If only it were that easy to remove all the harm they've done. Talk about an unholy trinity.

I need to tell Tony what I discovered. I strain to speak, but words won't come, as if the pearl won't allow them. Is it the pearl or is it me, not wanting to give up this secret power? Maybe both. It feels like the burden is mine until someone else becomes the Dragon Son and that someone needs a lot of convincing. I perch on the ottoman while Tony settles in his chair. "Um, you would've settled that better. I'm lousy at confrontation."

"You'll learn." He says in a way that suggests he's gonna teach me.

"No one respects me. Everyone thinks you're the boss already."

"They'll learn to think differently."

Yeah. Sure they will. Even if I'm willing to continue using the Yang Pearl to cheat my way to victory, that won't make me a natural-born leader like him. I can tell by the dark smudges under his eyes that the past few days have completely demoralized him. I wish I could take the time to coax him in the right direction, but this isn't that kind of decision. We need to settle this now.

"Um, I want you to know I don't blame you or Aaron for what..." I stop and swallow hard because I can't say Auntie Sylvia's name aloud. "For what she did."

"I should have believed you." His words drop like stones.

"And I should've understood why you didn't."

"This isn't on you, Little Brother. I could say I was blind to Mother's faults, but I wasn't. In the back of my mind, I wondered if what you'd said was true, because, if I'm honest, I knew what she was capable of." Tony blinks and I realize there are tears in his eyes. "I'm sorry," comes out as a choked whisper.

My heart sinks. I don't want him taking any blame for her. My nose tingles as my eyes fill with tears, too. "Big Brother, I knew you knew. I also knew you couldn't blame her without proof."

"Your word should have been enough."

But it wasn't. That one fact can forever drive a wedge between us, except it would mean that Auntie Sylvia wins. I won't allow that, though if Tony becomes Dragon Son, that also means she wins, right? No. He'll be Dragon Son despite her. My breath shakes out of me. "Look, no one else has to know." I mean that. I only ever wanted Tony and Aaron to believe me. "Um, I did text a copy of the letter to Auntie Cat, but only because she's got information we need to know. Sorry I didn't tell you first…" My voice trails off.

His expression becomes robotic as does his voice. "I have prepared copies of the letter to be sent to the clan elders."

My mouth drops open. What the fuck? "Why?"

"I want them to know Mother's crimes." Of course, he does. He'll scorch the earth as long as his righteousness is satisfied. "Also, the letter contains proof of that Head Elder and our uncle paid the Shinobi to kill our father."

I smack my forehead. How can he be so dense? "No, the letter contains proof that your mother was a liar, a cheater, and a murderer. Who's gonna believe anything else she says?"

"Some will."

Bullshit. I know what he's up to. Putting the brakes on anyone trying to make him the Dragon Son, including me. Son of a bitch. Literally! There's no point in damage control. All I can do is plow ahead, so I blurt out, "The Yin Pearl's been found."

Robot Tony is replaced by a human as he blinks. "What?"

"The Yin Pearl. I know where it is."

He scoots forward in his chair, frowning as if I'd told a bad joke. "What are you talking about? How is that possible?

Unless…" His expression changes like he's found religion as he whispers, "Did Jade Dragon guide you to it?"

"Him? No way." I'd asked Jade Dragon to help me find it so I could heal a mortally wounded John Walks Long and he refused. I was so angry at him, but now I wonder. Would taking the Yin Pearl have harmed or even killed Matthew? Did Jade Dragon save me from making an impossible choice? No. He likes hard choices and thinks they make you wise. The choices I have right now aren't any easier.

Tony listens while I tell him about Gerry and Matthew, and the Yin Pearl. When I finish, he sits back in his chair, shaking his head with wonder. "Jade Dragon must have arranged for you and Penny to meet so she could lead you to the Yin Pearl."

Right. Just wait 'til he gets a load of Jade Dragon, then he'll know better. Still, it doesn't hurt to have him think that. "Yeah, so I'm sure our ancestor will want us to help the Sparrows heal Matthew. Thing is, the power of the Yin and Yang Pearls can only merged by the Dragon Son and his wife. I'm not married, but you are, and we need to get the Yin Pearl back, so…"

I take the Yang Pearl from around my neck and hold it out to him. Tony stares at it like a mesmerized cat. I almost want to dangle it to see if he takes a swat. Instead, I hold my breath.

He shakes his head. "Even if I were willing, the answer would still be no. May is pregnant. The energy she would need to expend to heal Matthew would harm our unborn child."

Crap. That's right. I hadn't thought of that. "What are we going to do, then? The Wongs won't give us the pearl unless we heal Matthew."

"Then we must take it from them." And Robot Tony is back.

"Without healing him first?"

"They are members of the Two Dragon Clan and must make the necessary sacrifice."

"But they're not. Didn't you hear what I said. Head Elder

kicked them out. They have no protection. We need to help them right now."

"The best protection we can give them is taking the pearl so they are no longer a target."

I rub my forehead, trying to think through my frustration. "Okay, so, after the baby is born, will you and May use the pearls to heal Matthew?"

His face loses expression and his voice becomes ice. "No. I am not and will never be the Dragon Son."

I grit my teeth so I don't shout, 'Fucker!' Is his fucking righteousness worth more than someone's life? Except it's more than that. I can see it in his slumped shoulders and haunted eyes. He trusted and admired Dad more than anyone in the world, and he loved his mother despite all her faults. The wounds of betrayal are too deep. He can't be the Dragon Son. What gives meaning to his life now is fighting for me. If I love him and want to make up for the years I cut him off, I'll let him do that.

After my parents died, I renounced the title. Taking it back feels like betraying them and, almost worse, giving up all my hope for a free life on the Wayward Way. I can't be with Penny if I'm the Dragon Son and I can't save Matthew if I'm not. She'll do anything to save him. How can I deny her that? Tears fill my eyes again as my throat constricts. I swallow hard and rub my tingling nose. No time for tears. Only action matters now.

I stand and place the Yang Pearl around my neck. Warmth spreads through my chest as it activates my *chi*. My entire body tingles as energy races through my limbs before subsiding. I like this power. I want this power, which makes me realize the longer I wear this thing, the harder it will be for me to give it up.

Tony's eyes close as his shoulders sag with relief. Then he rises to his feet and looks on me with pride. "I know this isn't what you want, but it's the right thing to do. It's the only way we can defeat our enemies and take back our clan."

I wish I could make him understand how unimportant that is to me and that I'm doing this not only to help him, but to stop him from ruining Penny's family.

"Okay, my first act as Dragon Son is to mark your mother's letter confidential. We need to protect Aaron from the fallout."

Tony nods as if finally realizing he's not the only one that letter will scorch.

"My second act is to put you in charge of defeating Head Elder and Uncle George. So… um… come up with a plan and get back to me."

Pride becomes a more typical squint of frustration. "What do you mean?"

"I mean what I say. I'm the Dragon Son and I'm giving you an order. If you don't like it, say the word and the Yang Pearl is yours."

We lock eyes for a long time. I know he won't blink first, but since I'm the goddam Dragon Son, I can blink all I want, so I do, and head for the door. "Okay, I'm outta here."

"Where are you going?"

"The Dragon Son doesn't answer to anyone."

"You can't marry Penny."

I stop, but don't turn to face him so I won't say anything I'll regret. "It's our clan's fault that her father is dead. I won't let her stepfather die, too. Our honor is at stake." Tony can't wiggle out of that, even if he realizes I'm being manipulative. "I'm the Dragon Son, and we do things my way. End of story."

A thick silence fills the space between us. Neither one of us will budge, so I leave.

I get on my bike, but I can't make myself steer toward Penny and her family. I head back to my studio, but instead of going inside, I walk to the edge of the pier and sit with my legs dangling over the side. It's a rare, windless day and the bay more like a lake. The waves are motionless, which means Jade Dragon is far away.

Hope this is what you want because it's what you got, you asshole.

He doesn't answer, which is a good thing because it's not wise to cuss out a dragon. See, I am learning.

I sit here for a while, my fingers playing with the gritty mixture of wood and concrete. Finally, I take out my phone and text Penny.

> It's not good. Tony refuses to be the Dragon Son no matter what I say. I can't talk right now.

> It's okay. Bridie's too hung-over to deal. Call me when you're ready. We'll figure something out.

K

Except there's nothing to figure out. The only way we can use the pearls together is if we have sex, which will not only change everything between us, but I can't even do the honorable thing and marry her. I pound the edge of the pier, but all that gives me is splinters. I head into the warehouse. It's the quiet time of day when most of the artists are deep in their creations.

I busy myself sorting through my spray cans and stencils. I have a final piece of art I was going to paint on an alley wall in the Tenderloin where Jeremiah couldn't miss it. It's based on a famous photo from the Vietnam War of two men, one holding a gun at arm's length, pointed at the other dude's head. Beneath it, I was going to add the proverb, "Within the four seas all men are brothers." I never got around to it because, well, everything. Should I go out and do it tonight?

No. That's something Lennon would do, not the Dragon

Son. Shit. No. This can't be my life. I'm not giving up my art, my friends, everything I care about, just to lead a clan into battles that are meaningless to me.

I've got to find a way to have a choice in all this. Even though it's early, I go to bed because I'm fucking exhausted. Maybe when I wake up later tonight, I'll go out and throw up my tag somewhere to get it out of my system.

My buzzing phone jolts me awake. Morning light filters through the tinted ceiling windows and I can hear my fellow artists rambling around. I sit up, rub my dry eyes, and wince against a headache that demands water and coffee. My phone buzzes again. I grimace. I'm tempted to ignore it, except it might be... I check the screen. It is.

I know you said you can't talk, but can you
come over?

Something weird happened.

What?

Not something I can text about. Just come
over.

Is it an emergency? Are you in trouble?

No. Nothing like that. But it's something you
need to see.

I clench the phone in my fist. What has Tony done now?

Lennon

Penny buzzes me in and meets me at her front door. She's still wearing pajamas and looks like she just woke from a nightmare. She grabs a hunk of her hair and tugs at it while she speaks. "Hi. Um, sorry, I didn't mean to be mysterious, but, um…"

"Is that Lennon?" Bridie calls out from the kitchen, her voice like a creaking door.

I reach out and touch Penny's mind. She opens and I ask, *Is she drunk again?*

No. I poured all the booze down the sink while she slept it off.

Is she mad?

That's not the kind of thing that makes her mad.

So, what's going on?

She takes a deep breath. *I didn't tell you because I didn't want you to be angry while you drove here. It's in the kitchen.*

What is?

Your aunt's jewelry box.

I stare because I can't speak, silently or otherwise. Then I stride past her to the kitchen. Auntie Sylvia's jewelry box looms in the center of the table, rose-scented misery pouring out like invisible smoke. Bridie stares at it while pooling a strand of pearls in and out of her palm while Kai pokes through the contents with a spoon.

Nausea clogs my throat as if someone punched me in the gut. No, not someone. Tony.

Penny comes up beside me, still tugging her hair. "It, um… it came with a note."

Bridie's bright green glare fixes on me. "What is your cousin playing at?" She tosses the pearls and they skitter across the table before falling on the floor. No one moves to pick them up. She grabs a sheet of paper and waves it at me. "You should read this… this…" She huffs and reads aloud.

Mrs. Sparrow, Lennon has explained how our clan has wronged your family. I apologize that I am unable to help you in your present difficulty. Lennon is the Dragon Son and cannot aid you until he is married, which could be several years from now. Please use the proceeds from this box to care for your husband until then. In the meantime, we require that the Yin Pearl be returned to us.

"We require. Bloody hell!" She crushes the note, her face bright red. Tears fill her eyes. "He can take his blood money and shove it up his arse."

I chew my lip, break open the scab and taste blood. Pain punctures my red haze of fury. I speak through a tight throat. "Can I see the note?"

She tosses it at me, snatches up the pearls and works at them like Auntie Cat does with her rosary when she's anxious.

I smooth out the paper and stare at the words, not at what they say but how they're written. Tony's normal handwriting is as precise as he is. These words are jagged and hurried as if the note were a necessary afterthought and not the product of a clear head. I exhale, releasing some of my anger. Then I take out my phone. The Sparrows have a right to know what-the-fuck, but I don't need them watching and listening right now. I brush past Penny and head for the front room. She doesn't follow.

Tony answers, "Dragon Son."

Even now he's got to hammer that home. "Why?"

"I wanted to throw that box into the gutter but May convinced me it's better karma to put it to good use. The Sparrows can sell the jewelry and use the proceeds to keep Matthew safe and in good care until you're ready to heal him."

I chew my lip again because I need the pain to keep from shouting. "She murdered my mother and now her jewelry box is sitting on my best friend's kitchen table. How do you think that makes me feel?"

Moments pass, and Tony doesn't answer. And it hits me, he sent the jewelry box to the Sparrows without thinking it through. Tony does nothing without considering every possible outcome, but this time he did. Wow. Maybe he really can't be Dragon Son, at least not right now, because however bad my emotional baggage is, his is worse.

"I'm sorry," he whispers. No excuses because that's something else he never does.

"Big Brother, I'll deal with it. Right now, I need you to come up with a strategy to defeat our uncle. Leave the Sparrows to me and don't interfere." I hang up and put my phone on silent mode because I don't want to hear whatever else he has to say.

I close my eyes and focus on the Yang Pearl. Before Dad died, he'd trained me in its use, tapping its power in large and small doses. A large dose fills you with amazing power, but almost immediately drains away and leaves you spent. A small dose can re-energize your *chi*, allowing you to extend your own power. As I do so, I can hear Dad's voice, explaining it all. It's painful, remembering a time when I didn't hate him. I push that thought away and allow Jade Dragon's energy to flush away my rage so I can think straight. Then I open my eyes and head back to the kitchen.

Penny stands over the jewelry box, dangling a diamond necklace between pinched fingers. "What the hell does he think we're going to do with all this?"

Bridie raises exasperated hands. "He must think Strowlers have ways of selling off ill-gotten goods."

Kai stares at the emerald ring on his pinky. "We do."

I clear my throat and they all look up. Penny releases the necklace while Kai tugs off the ring and tosses it back in the box. "I talked to Tony. He apologized. He wasn't thinking straight." Close enough, I guess. "But the note, yeah, that's the situation. He refuses to be the Dragon Son, so it's gotta be me."

Bridie covers her mouth and gives a little sob. Penny crosses her arms and looks down. Kai gives me a leery up-and-down look, as if considering whether to challenge me for his sister's honor.

Tony. I want to blame him for this, but I can't. I always thought Big Brother was made of steel and could take any blow. It's not on him that my expectations were unrealistic. This is my problem and I have to solve it, but how?

Bridie's hand slips from her face and she takes a deep breath. "I have to walk the labyrinth. "

My brother and I groan. I roll my eyes before saying, "Mum, the last time you walked the labyrinth, your answer was to marry Bill and move to San Francisco and look how that turned out."

"You wouldn't have met Lennon if we hadn't moved here. You know how it works. The fairies don't give direct answers." She pauses, looking down before continuing. "I never told you, but before I met your father, I walked the labyrinth and asked Leannán Sidhe to help me leave my family without being trapped by another. She told me the only way to leave my family was to marry the boy with a secret writ in his soul. When Gerry came to our Nest, I knew he was that boy."

"But his secret was he was gay."

"Yes. And marrying him led me to London, where I met Matthew. I walked the labyrinth again, this time with him at my side, and asked Leannán Sidhe if he was my one true love. She said yes." Her eyes mist over and her voice chokes. "He was my true love and the father of my next child."

Kai's eyes widen. "Really, Mum? Leannán Sidhe said that?"

She nods as if she can't speak and reaches over to squeeze his hand.

What can I say to that? Walking the labyrinth is a sacred thing, and the answers received are private, held close to the heart. Bridie's answers sound more like a string of coincidences, but maybe the fairies work through coincidences. Or they just like messing with mortals and seeing what happens. Regardless, if it moves things forward, it's all good. "Let's do it. Do you need my help?"

"Since this involves you and Lennon, I'll need you both."

Lennon's perplexed squint is almost funny. "What are we doing?"

"It's a Strowler thing." I try to think of the best way to explain it to him. "Walking the labyrinth is one of our second sight abilities. We consider labyrinths to be portals to the unseen world where the fairies reside. So, first you draw or build the labyrinth. Then, you walk it while chanting *oosha, aisha, laiasha, merai.*"

"What does that mean?"

"No idea. I mean, no one knows. It's fairy tongue. Anyway, when you reach the center, you pour out your offering, and make your plea to Leannán Sidhe."

"Offering?"

While we speak, Bridie opens the fridge and pours milk into a small bowl. Then she plucks a knife off the magnetic wall strip and beckons us to join her.

"Don't worry. She only needs a drop," I say to his widened eyes. We join her at the counter, where she pricks our left ring fingers. "We believe this finger contains the vein closest to the heart."

"Does it though?" he asks before sticking his finger in his mouth.

I shrug because biology wasn't a strong subject for me in school.

Bridie ignores us, using the knife to swirl our drops of blood into the milk, turning it light pink. Then she hands the bowl to me and nods for us to follow her.

We head downstairs, Kai on our heels, not about to miss the show. I feel the tickle of Lennon's mind and open up to him.

Do you really believe this?

Yeah, I guess. I mean, I believe in fairies the same way you believe in dragons. I was taught to draw and walk a labyrinth like any Strowler girl.

Have you?

No. I pause, not sure how to explain my reluctance. *Fairies are fickle and tempestuous. I'm not eager putting my fate in their hands, but this could get us closer to saving Matthew.*

Fairies sound a lot like dragons.

Are you okay with this?

Sure. I mean, if it cools Bridie's jets, it'll be good.

Exactly.

We enter the basement and pass the wire cages the tenants use for extra storage. Bridie unlocks the backdoor. It opens to a small backyard the landlord allows no one to access, except the property manager. Not for our use or enjoyment, but to maintain. Maintenance means mowing the patchy strip of lawn and trimming the sparse, scrubby bushes. Bridie secretly planted lavender, sage, and rosemary to summon a bit of magic into the sad landscape. Even now, in late fall, their blue and purple flowers bloom.

Bridie instructs me to sprinkle a bit of each herb into the bowl. While I do that, she pulls a tarp off the square gravel patio, revealing a small labyrinth carved into its depths.

"When did you do that?" I ask.

She shrugs, as if revealing a guilty secret. "The night we came back from London. I couldn't sleep, so I came out here. I begged Leannán Sidhe for help and she told me to wait."

She could say the same thing now, but I keep that to myself.

I hand Bridie the bowl and she begins her walk, gravel crunching beneath her feet as she takes small steps on the winding path. Her voice sounds tentative at first, but gains strength as she chants, *"Oosha, aisha, laiasha, merai."*

I glance at the boys on either side of me as they watch her solemnly. I wonder if, like me, they're wrestling with hope and skepticism. A light breeze blows through our dismal yard, bringing with it the scent of lavender, rosemary, and sage, all distinct and odd because I've never smelled them so strongly before.

Bridie reaches the center of the labyrinth and, still chanting, tips the bowl. The ground absorbs the thick pinkish liquid, including the herbs we added.

It's starts raining, not water, but silver sparkles that linger in the air like fireflies. Without thought, I reach for Lennon and Kai's icy hands, and chant, *"Oosha, aisha, laiasha, merai."*

They join me, but only for a few moments. We stop because she's here.

Leannán Sidhe.

I don't see her, but I feel her. Blood of my blood. Silver and dirt, wisdom and chaos. Not of this earth, and yet this earth gives her life. I squeeze the boys' hands and they squeeze back, letting me know they feel her, too.

Bridie bows her head, eyes closed, her hair seeming aflame.

I don't breathe. I can't. The silver sparkles fade and Leannán Sidhe slips away, back to the unseen world. I let go of the boys' hands and flex my crunched fingers. It's as if we were all holding on for dear life.

Bridie lifts her head, her curls back to golden red, though her eyes sparkle like emeralds. Tears glisten on her cheeks. Without a word, she winds her way back out of the labyrinth. Then she hands me the bowl and motions for Kai to help her with the tarp.

I gnaw my lip as they lay bricks on the tarp to keep it from blowing away. Lennon's feet crunch gravel as he shifts, his arms crossing his chest. Bridie turns away, heading for the door.

"Mum," I call after her. "What did Leannán Sidhe say?"

"I'll tell you when we're inside." Bridie doesn't look back.

"So, not good?" Lennon asks me.

Maybe. Or more likely, not the answer she wants.

Back in the kitchen, Bridie picks up the strand of pearls, working her fingers through them again, while gazing out the window without a word.

I give an impatient huff. "Mum."

"Leannán Sidhe said that you and Lennon…" She heaves a deep sigh. "Your fates are tied. I'm not to interfere. That only you two can save Matthew."

I exchange glances with Lennon. Our fates are tied? That's not really a surprise, but it's weird hearing it from a fairy. As for being the only ones who can save Matthew… No pressure. But at least Bridie will stop hounding Tony and let me and Lennon get on with it.

The pearls clatter on the table as she drops them. "So. We move to Plan B."

"There's a Plan B?" Kai asks with a pinched brow.

Of course, there is. Bridie is the Queen of Scheme. I should've known she was hatching plots while nursing her hangover. Problem is, most of her ideas are quick fixes that don't solve the problem. I can't summon much enthusiasm when I say, "Which is?"

She sucks in her breath before putting on a smile as false as Sylvia's diamonds are real. "Handfasting."

I groan and look up at the ceiling, rolling my eyes. "Pants!"

Lennon looks from me to her. "Is that something bad?"

"Not at all," says Bridie. "Handfasting is common among Strowlers who wed young. It's a marriage that lasts a year and a day. The couple then decides whether to stay together for good or call it quits. If they separate, the marriage dissolves and the girl's family keeps the dowry."

"So, you mean me and Penny…"

"Exactly. Handfasting protects your honor, but isn't as binding as marriage." She rubs her chin with the back of her hand. "The hard part will be convincing Christy."

I scoff. "You think?"

"What's he got to do with it?" asks Lennon.

Bridie replies, "Handfasting is only legitimate when performed by the Upright Man."

"Will Christy do it?"

I scoff again and give a flat, "No."

Bridie glares at me. "You don't know that."

"Yeah, I do. How are you going to convince him?"

"By offering him a dowry he can't refuse."

We all look at the jewelry box.

"Uncle Christy loves gelt," Kai tells Lennon.

"He can have it all," says our mother. "I'd pay any amount to heal Matthew and not compromise your honor."

Okay, now I'm getting pissed. "It's my honor. Why does anyone think they have anything to say about it?"

Bridie groans. "You still don't understand the world we live in."

"The world you live in." My hands go to my hips "You used to walk the Wayward Way and not care about that crap or what Christy thinks. You changed. Not me. I'm still on the Wayward Way and I'll do what I want."

"Of course you don't care." Bridie juts her chin at Lennon. "You have a man to watch over you. For now. Once he scarpers, you're done for. Your honor will be in ruins and then you'll see how hard life can be."

"I won't scarper." Lennon's brow furrows. "Whatever that means." He turns to Kai. "Right?"

My brother gives him stink-eye. "You better not, man."

This is going nowhere. I grab my non-scarpering friend's hand. "Lennon and I need to talk. In private."

Bridie's mouth and eyes become thin lines of frustration. If she could turn into a fly, she'd be buzzing after us as we head to my bedroom.

I slam the door shut, lean against it and groan. "I can't believe she came up with that. Well, no, I can. It's Bridie." I gaze at Lennon's pensive face. "Sorry."

"It's okay." He shrugs. "Tony's still trying to run my life. Why wouldn't Bridie be trying to run yours?"

I sigh out the word "Exactly." I'm knackered from dealing with all the emotional turmoil. Lennon must be, too. I nod my head and he follows me to the bed, where we sit cross-legged, facing each other. I hug a pillow to my chest.

Lennon reaches for a pillow, too. "So, the labyrinth. That was a trip. I guess I believe in fairies now."

"Yeah, they're real but," I shrug. "Don't mess with them, don't ask much of them, and you'll be fine."

"They really do sound like dragons." The Clash album I gave him for his birthday slides out from where he left it. His fingers skim the surface. "So, this handfasting thing, would it be so bad?"

I hug the pillow a little tighter. "In theory, no. It'd be the perfect answer, but only if you were a Strowler or if Christy were an Upright Man on the Wayward Way. He'll never do it, not for any price. He loves gelt, but he values his honor more. If Bridie asks him to handfast us, he'll think we've been dallying and see that as a stain on his family's honor."

"Has she told him about the pearls?"

"No, but she will. She'll say anything to get her way. Not that it matters. He won't believe her. He'll think the pearls are some kind of trick."

"No one else can know about the pearls. The more people who know, the more likely Uncle George will find out."

"I know. Don't worry. I'll set her straight. We're not getting handfasted."

"So, what do we do?"

"I'm open to suggestions."

He tucks his pillow under his chin. "What about a secret wedding?"

"Secret wedding? You mean, like Romeo and Juliet."

"No. I mean, yeah, but not like in the play. That ended bad. Anyway, we get married, go to London, do what we gotta do, and come back here."

'Do what we gotta do' is so loaded, I don't want to think about it. "But it's an extra step we don't have to take and will cause a lot of trouble. We don't have to get married."

He shakes his head, his brown eyes now more hawk than owl. "It's not only your honor, Penny. It's my honor, too. I need to do what I think is right and I won't feel right about this if we're not married."

He's right. It's not all about me. I hadn't considered his feelings. Our world is built on honor and embedded in our DNA. It's not scraped off that easy. I think of honor as a trap, but that doesn't mean I've escaped it. "Okay, let's do it. If Uncle Christy finds out, Bridie can give him the jewelry box. It might not help, but it won't hurt."

We stare at each other across our pillows. He gives a tight shrug. "Not real romantic, huh?"

"Not so much."

"Should I get down on one knee?"

"Please don't."

We both grin because it's all so ridiculous, but also deadly serious. As our smiles fade, Lennon says, "I wish we could chuck that box into the bay."

"Me, too. It feels like a bad omen." A queen's fortune and nobody wants a dime. Or diamond. "So, what next? I mean, do you know how to use the pearls together?"

Lennon squeezes the pillow to his chest. "Sorta? We have stories about the Dragon Son and his wife performing the Dragon Touch."

"Real stories or fairy tales?"

"Both?"

That fills me with confidence. "Okay. Well, did they heal lots of people?"

"No. That's the thing about the Dragon Touch. There's a catch."

"There always is."

"This one's pretty bad. So, the Dragon Son's Wife used the Yin Pearl for *chi* healing. That's when she lays her hands on someone and channels her *chi* through the pearl to amplify its energy. It doesn't heal like…" He pauses trying to think of a comparison.

"Like Jesus healing?"

"Yeah. Not like that. It's more like giving the injured person more energy to heal on their own. It's great for, like, a broken rib or a bruised kidney. The Dragon Touch is kinda like Jesus healing, except the Yin Pearl absorbs the illness. The Dragon Son's Wife can't use it again, for any kind of healing, until she expels the illness into another person."

My eyes widen. "Whoa. That is bad."

"Yeah. They tried expelling the illness into animals, but it didn't work. Has to be a human."

"So, what did they do?"

"They expelled the illnesses into their enemies, but because of bad karma, they couldn't do it to just anyone. It had to be someone who was threatening their lives."

"So, what if there's still an illness trapped in the pearl right now?"

"There isn't. The story goes that toward the end of the Taiping Rebellion, the Dragon Son and his wife became disillusioned with the Heavenly King and used the Dragon Touch to expel an illness into him that eventually killed him. The Heavenly King still had the Wisdom Pearl and felt what they'd done. They escaped and hid their children, and the Yin and Yang pearls, with Christian missionaries. Then they lured away their enemies on a chase until they were caught and killed."

My eyes narrow. "Is that a story or what actually happened?"

He lifts his hands as he shrugs. "Guess we'll find out when we get to London."

"All we have to do is get married and get there on the down low."

"Yeah."

"Yeah." We're both silent while pondering that. One thing is obvious. "Well, it's Halloween, so I guess we could disguise ourselves, and…" My pillow drops to the floor as I gasp and grasp his knee. "Monstrosity!"

"What about it?"

"We can volunteer to help Junkyard Metallurgy with their giant spider. Then we can sneak away in the middle of Monstrosity, and then, I don't know…" I snap my fingers as the idea hits me. "Fly to Vegas and get married, and then head for London."

His lower lip puffs out as he mulls my words. "Yeah, I guess, but won't it seem weird we're dropping everything to go to a Halloween party?"

"Not if we're stupid about it. I mean, make everyone think we're doing it so we can be together. We can say that before all the trouble started, we gave Junkyard Metallurgy our word we'd help them. It sounds lame, but it's supposed to."

"We are doing it so we can be together."

"So, we'll be very convincing."

"And we get to be together."

"Exactly."

We smile at each other and I get that feeling like I'm with my only ally, the one person who won't let me down. Then his mind touches mine. I shiver as chills run through me. The sensation makes me feel so much closer to him, like I'm with my soulmate who I can never give up.

You're really okay about all this? he asks.

Yeah. Sorry I'm being so weird about, you know, the sex stuff. I just… I don't feel ready yet.

It's okay. Me, neither. I don't want anything to change. Between us, I mean. I always want to be your friend.

Same. That'll never change.

He leans across his pillow and kisses me. I close my eyes as our lips touch and linger. The scab on his lip tastes of blood and is for some odd reason really sexy. I want him to touch me. I want to touch him. Our mutual sigh parts us. I pick up my pillow and hug it tight. "I'll tell Bridie. She loves a good scheme and could be helpful."

"I can't tell Tony. I can act angry and irresponsible for a couple more days before he gets on my case again." He rubs his forehead. "And I still have some questions that need answers before we go anywhere."

"Do you know who has the answers?"

"Yeah. Auntie Cat."

Lennon

Auntie Cat lives on Irving Street, close to Golden Gate Park and far from Chinatown. I used to wonder why she lived out here and almost never came to the *kongsi*. Now I know. She couldn't stand watching in silence while her brothers and Auntie Sylvia deceived everyone. I don't blame her for running away. I ran away, too.

I park in front of her building and the first thing I see is the CLOSED sign on the glass door of her martial arts studio. My stomach drops. When my parents died, she dropped everything, including the studio, to take care of me. After we moved back to SF from Seattle, she reopened her business. Now, thanks to me and her shitty brothers, she's closed it again. I should've talked to her before now. She doesn't deserve my harshness. She was my age when Dad forced her to swear an oath of silence. Would I have stood up against him? I'd like to think so, but if I'm honest, I know better.

I head upstairs, unlock the door, and take off my shoes. Auntie Cat steps out of the kitchen and into the hallway, blinking in surprise at the sight of me.

"Lennon. I'm… I'm… so glad you came home." She stammers through a relieved smile that barely touches the sorrow in her eyes.

Uncle Roy leans out the door and gives me a cautious nod.

I nod back. "Hi. I'm here to pick up a few things."

"We're making lunch," says Auntie Cat. "Sandwiches. Why don't you join us? I'll make your favorite."

My stomach doesn't rumble, but my heart nudges me because that sandwich is my comfort food, so I nod again. I'm not ready to talk yet, so I head to my room. I work fast, digging up my passport and grabbing clothes, all of which get stuffed into a backpack. I can't take much since I don't want to look like I'm packing for a trip. When I'm done, I glance around the room one last time. I haven't spent much time here, so it doesn't carry the emotional weight of my bedroom in the *kongsi* where I grew up, or even the one in Seattle, where I spent two years brooding over my grief and rage. The walls here are bare, since all my art is in my studio, and the only personal item that catches my eye is the watch Tony gave me for my birthday.

I pick it up and run my thumb over its ridged black metal band. It's an actual watch, with a face and hands rather than a screen, and a Swiss name I can't pronounce. It's everything-proof, has a compass and a barometer, and is sort of cool except I hate it. Not because it's from Tony, but because of the Chinese proverb he had engraved on the back.

Tiger father begets tiger son

Yeah, I'll bet he's regretting that now. I almost toss it on my bed, but somehow, I can't. It's weird, but I want something of Tony to come with me. Everything that's about to happen affects him as much as me. We're in this together even if we can't agree on anything.

I open my closet and take out the sheath that holds my throwing knives. I pull one out and scrape the sharp edge across the watch's metal back. It hurts, like I'm scraping Dad off my soul, but can only scratch away the surface. He'll always be there, but I don't have to look at him. I rub away the fragments and strap on the watch. It feels like a cuff, like a reminder that wherever I go, I'll never be free.

I leave my room and drop my backpack in the hall before entering the kitchen. Auntie Cat and Uncle Roy are sitting at the kitchen table, half-eaten sandwiches before them. I drop into my chair and this time my stomach rumbles when I look at my plate. Right after we moved to Seattle, Auntie Cat had asked me what I wanted for lunch. I rattled off an assortment of food. She brought me a sandwich with all of it: toasted wheat bread, peanut butter, honey, trail mix, and potato chips. I know that sounds gross, but it tastes so good. She'd been trying to make me smile, and it worked then. Not today, but I still dig in.

After a few bites, I say, "You read the letter."

They nod. Auntie Cat adds, "It fills in some holes."

I set down my sandwich. "Like what?"

"Neither of us knew Mike planned to make Tony his heir," says Roy.

"Do you know if my mom knew?"

"No, but if Mike gave her the Yang Pearl, she probably did."

That's what I thought, but I guess I'll never know for sure.

"Also, Sylvia's cancer," says Auntie Cat. "The diagnosis came so soon after your parents died. I wondered if she was faking it for sympathy until she showed symptoms. It makes sense that Head Elder was punishing her with a slow, painful death."

"You knew why she hated Mom. Why didn't you believe me up when I said she killed her?"

Auntie Cat covers her mouth and looks down for a moment before she speaks again. "Because if Sylvia was going to kill your mother, she would've done it while Mike was alive and able to marry her and make Tony legitimate. Fear of Head Elder always stood in her way. Plus, the hatred between George and Sylvia got worse as Tony got older. George deeply resented that Tony wasn't his son. He and Sylvia never would've worked together and Head Elder would never order his daughter's murder. I couldn't understand what would motivate Sylvia to kill your mother at that moment. Now I know. The Yang Pearl."

Only Head Elder believed me. He knew what Sylvia was capable of because he's just as ruthless. Auntie Cat and Uncle Roy are like Tony, unable to compromise their honor regardless of what's at stake. Am I like them? I should be, but I'm not. I proved that when I ran away and took up a life of crime. I always thought being Dad's son made me honorable by default, but now I think the opposite is true. Whatever made him dishonorable and capable of deception is part of me, too. Much as I hate him for it, I'm glad. Otherwise, I wouldn't be scheming with Penny to runaway and heal Matthew, regardless of how that affects the Two Dragon Clan.

Cat and Roy exchange glances during my silence. Then she says, "It's not just the Yang Pearl that's at stake."

"What?" My heart starts pounding. Do they know about the Yin Pearl? Has the secret gotten out?

"You know that George is a scholar and he's been trained to recognize the missing pearls."

Shit.

She takes a shaky breath before continuing. "Twenty years ago, during a trip to London, the Knights Templar invited Mike, George, and my parents to visit their secret compound. They were give a tour of the chamber containing the Knights' sacred relics, mostly looted weapons of war. Among the Opium War relics, George found a dagger with a large pearl embedded in its hilt. After close inspection, he realized it was the Wisdom Pearl."

My mouth drops open. No. Way. This is huge. How could I not know? "The Wisdom Pearl was found?"

She holds up her hand to silence me. "Rather than wait and let our father handle it, George took the dagger and ran, leaving Mike and my parents to face the consequences. He was caught and dragged before the Templar's Grandmaster, who condemned him to death. He swung his sword at George, but my mother stepped in and the Grandmaster killed her instead."

Auntie Cat stops and looks up at the ceiling before taking a deep breath. I know how she feels. It still hurts like it was yesterday, even years later. Uncle Roy takes her hand. She squeezes before she lets go and takes another deep breath.

"The Templars claimed they regretted her death and allowed Dad and my brothers to leave the compound with the dagger. When they returned to the London *kongsi*, Dad knew he had to put the Wisdom Pearl someplace beyond temptation for him or anyone else. He ordered a vault and placed it inside. Only he and Mike knew the combination."

"Wait. So, you're saying the Wisdom Pearl has been in a safe in London for the past twenty years?"

"Yes, but that's not the end of the story."

Cat

I was forbidden entrance to Chisel Knife Mountain until after my father died. His wives were dead, too, and everyone seemed eager to sweep their transgressions under the rug. That I was a product of those transgressions became less a point of contention, though his First Wife's family still refused to see me as legitimate. The elders denied me the right to train at my ancestral home, but no one protested when Michael included me as a guest at his wedding. At least, not that I knew of.

My mouth dropped open when I first stepped through the front entrance and into the main courtyard, gawking at the sturdy stone walls and towers built to surround the entrance to our sacred caverns. I felt like everyone was staring at me, The Girl, as my not-stepmother Tiffany called me. I wanted to use the Stealth Skill to skulk along the walls like a shameful shadow, but Chelle, Mike's fiancé, linked arms with me while he led the way through the compound to our Ancestral Hall.

Candlelight flickered off the cavern walls and huge coils of incense hung from the ceiling, ends burning amber-red as their ash dropped to the floor. The heady scent of sandalwood and candle wax, continuously burning for over 500 years, hung thick in the air and enveloped me as I sensed our ancestors all around us. We stopped before Jade Dragon's altar and I gazed for the first time on his spirit tablet and Summoning Pearl embedded within. I could feel his presence, not close, but somewhere in the South China Sea, watching the continuous stream of massive container ships heading to and from ports in Hong Kong and Shenzhen. The pollution they left in their wake was poisoning a pod of dolphins, and Jade Dragon swished his tail to disperse the toxic ooze.

Mike lit three sticks of incense and held them out to me with questioning eyes. After Dad died, I left the *kongsi* to live in a dorm at UC Berkeley. I was done with the Two Dragon Clan and to prove it, I converted to Catholicism. However, the church I attended was liberal and my priest encouraged converts to hold on to their cultures while embracing their new faith. This was definitely part of my culture. I took the incense, and for the first time in my life, bowed before Jade Dragon. He was too busy with the dolphins to notice, which was fine. I didn't want him to notice me, anyway.

"I have a surprise for you," Mike said as we left the cavern and walked across the interior courtyard.

My shoulders tensed. The way he says it, I'm pretty sure what, or rather, who, it is. Was he really that insensitive? Or was he hoping to make something happen again, thinking enough time had passed? Would that much time ever pass? I didn't know.

He winked and Chelle smiled as she took the hand he held out. I frowned behind their backs. That last summer, I'd hung out with Chelle when she came to San Francisco to get acquainted with Mike. We'd bonded as she told me about her heart condition, her father's threats to disown her if she didn't produce an heir at the right time, and her bewilderment at Sylvia's contempt. I wanted so badly to tell her of Mike and Sylvia's affair, but an oath sealed my lips. Chelle confessed through blushes that she and Mike had been intimate. It was hard not to roll my eyes. Of course, he seduced her. At least, from the look on Chelle's face, he'd been kinder and gentler to her than he had to Sylvia.

They led me into another courtyard and upstairs to the formal residence of the Dragon Son and his family. Or at least it was until Dad took up permanent residence in San Francisco with Mike and my mother. Tiffany stayed here with George as was her right as the Dragon Son's First Wife. I hesitated at the threshold despite Mike's assurance that he'd had the place refurnished, repainted, and cleansed by a *feng shui* master after she died. When I finally entered, a chill crept up my spine as I imagined her brooding, plotting, and cursing the man who'd left her for another woman.

"Your luggage is in your room," Mike said as we took off our shoes.

I hoped that was a cue because I really wanted to sleep off my jet lag, but we headed down the hall toward the living room. There, sitting on the couch, was my surprise.

My eyelids fluttered and my cheeks flushed as Roy rose from the couch and towered over us all.

"Hey, Cat," he rumbled with a casual shrug.

"Hey." I shrugged back as if my heart wasn't hammering. As if I didn't still love him, even though I hadn't seen him in almost three years. Not since my darkest moment, my hour of need, when he'd chosen loyalty to Mike over me. I couldn't forgive him then. Could I now?

Mike clapped him on the back. "Chelle and I have to go to my office to look over some paperwork. How about you show my sister around the compound?"

Roy nodded and looked at me with cautious eyes. "Sure, if Cat's up for it."

I didn't want to be. I wanted to tell him I was too tired, but my head nodded at the prompting of my heart.

A little boy came bounding into the room as he called out, "Auntie Cat."

I opened my arms, lifted and swung him around in a hug. He peered at me with those always solemn eyes and accepted my kiss on the cheek.

"He's been talking about you all day," said Chelle. She smiled as Tony held out his arms for her to take him.

"Son, no, don't bother her," came Sylvia's sharp voice from the doorway. She barged in between me and Chelle and yanked her son away, almost scraping him with the manila envelope tucked under one arm.

I grimaced at her scent of roses mingled with jealousy. Much as I loved my nephew, I wished Sylvia and George would move out of the *kongsi*. George wanted to live in Hong Kong, in the mansion on the Peak he'd inherited when his mother died. He was even willing to move to a ritzier San Francisco address, but Sylvia refused. She'd stated she wanted to live in the *kongsi* so Tony would have the benefit of the finest martial arts training possible. The real reason was she wanted Mike to feel guilty about how he'd treated her. He knew it, I knew it, and so did Roy.

The one person none of us could ever tell came striding in, arms wide open. "Cat."

I accepted George's hug, even though he was responsible for my mother's death. He'd behaved stupidly, even cowardly, but it hadn't been his intention. Plus, I had my guilt to deal with. My revenge against George was swearing to silence about Mike and Sylvia's affair. I wished I'd broken that oath because if I had, she wouldn't be a part of our family.

His hands settled on my shoulders. "Finally here, huh? I'm sorry they had kept you away all these years, but we'll make it up to you, right, Mike?" He glanced at our brother, who nodded. "We'll take you on a tour of the caverns. It's your right. You are a Dragon Son's daughter."

My eyes widened, and I turned to Mike, who nodded again, only this time he was smiling, too. Finally, I was going to see the caverns that held the secret knowledge of our clan. Only the Dragon Son's family, the clan elders, and a chosen handful of historians and guards were allowed inside. The deaths of our parents really had removed the stain of my birth.

A brittle smile cracked Sylvia's tense face as if she was trying hard to pretend she gave a damn. Then she handed Tony to Michelle. "Put my son down for his nap. Please. I need to talk to the family in private."

My mouth dropped open. I turned to Mike, who looked away. Why did he let that bitch talk to his future wife like she's the maid? Okay, I knew why, but I didn't have that problem. "Chelle is part of our family, too."

"Not. Yet." The two words gritted between Sylvia's overly whitened teeth.

Tony heaved a sigh and snuggled his head into the crook of Chelle's neck, as if he could finally relax. Her eyes softened, and she said, "It's all right. I'll take him."

Mike's eyes softened, too, at the sight of a child in the arms of his future wife. He kissed her cheek and patted Tony's head before they walked out the door.

Sylvia watched his actions with razor eyes. She closed the door with a sharp click before slitting the rest of us with her gaze. "No, stay," she snapped when Roy moved toward the door. "This concerns you, too."

Dread pooled in my stomach as I realized what she was about to say. This was it, her last chance to stop Michael's wedding, and Sylvia seized opportunity the same way she grasped diamonds and pearls. I'm not an actor. I couldn't make myself look stupidly curious or startled. All I could do was maintain the blank expression I'd used to hide my feelings for my entire life.

George crossed his arms, tilted his head, and chuckled.

"What is it, Syl? Do you want to host a party or something? I'm sure Chelle won't care."

Sylvia's nostrils flared. She locked eyes with Mike, who was expressionless except for his icy stare. Hesitancy crossed her face because she knew, better than me, how cold-blooded he could be. Then her gaze sharpened again as she turned to George. "Husband, I had an affair with the Dragon Son. It lasted from the time I arrived in San Francisco until our wedding."

Everything went still for a moment that seemed to last a thousand years.

George looked as if she'd punched him in the throat.

Mike shook his head.

Her eyes fixed on him as she said, "Cat and Roy are my witnesses. They caught us in the act."

It took all my willpower not to flinch.

"Is this true?" George asked me in a whisper.

I shook my head, mute, because I didn't want to lie aloud. Roy did the same.

Sylvia huffed as if hyperventilating. "Michael swore them to secrecy, but they know the truth." She jabbed her finger at us with each of the last four words.

Mike's head dropped as he heaved a long sigh. Then he looked up, looked our brother in the eyes, and lied. "Remember how drunk we got at your bachelor party? I was so plastered I needed help finding my hotel room. I can't even remember getting into bed, but I somehow did, and found a girl waiting there. It was dark, so I couldn't see her and, to be honest, I didn't care. I thought she was a gift from you, so I rolled with it. When I woke up the next day, I discovered it was Sylvia. She'd snuck into my bed to trick me into having sex with her. She tried to blackmail me, but I didn't fall for it."

Sylvia's pale cheeks reddened before the words choked out of her, "That's not true."

George watched them, expressionless, his fists clenched at his side. Then he turned to me and Roy. "Is it true?"

It was a relief I could honestly say, "I don't know."

Roy shook his head. "I don't know, either. Mike never told me."

"I told no one." Mike jut his chin at Sylvia. "I was trying to protect her honor."

"Honor?" George choked out as he turned to his twin. "What about my honor? You should've told me. I wouldn't have married her."

"You think you had a choice? Mother would've swept it all under the rug and made you marry her, anyway."

George blinked once at that undeniable truth. He turned to his wife, but before he could speak, she whipped out the envelope from under her arm and pulled out two forms, which she shoved into my brothers' hands. "DNA tests showing my son's true father."

I gasped aloud. "What?" No. I couldn't believe Mike had been so careless.

My brothers scanned their papers. Then George looked up and whispered, "This says I'm not Tony's father."

"And this says I am." Mike glared at Sylvia. "I didn't submit to a DNA test, so how…"

"Your hair. I took hair from both your brushes." Her arms folded tight despite her triumphant smile.

"I see," Mike's mouth twisted with a cruel smirk. "And we're supposed to believe that you didn't switch our samples? We're supposed to believe a slut who sleeps around to get what she wants?" He turned to George. "She's trying to keep me from marrying Michelle. That's what this is all about. She wants me to marry her so she can be the Dragon Son's Wife."

Tears glittered like broken glass in her eyes. "Yes. I want my rightful place. I will claim my son's heritage and you can't stop me."

"This," Mike dangled the lab results in her face, "is bullshit. For all we know, these are forgeries and there was never any test. But let's say it's real and I am Tony's father. You think Head Elder will set aside his daughter? Before that happens, he'll see you disgraced, shamed, cast out of our clan. Your family will lose face and reject you and Tony. Do you want that? Do you want to raise your son in the gutter?"

"Your father had two wives. Why can't you?"

George sputtered with indignation. My mouth dropped open. How could she even think such a thing? My father married the woman he loved, not his brother's wife.

"You know why I'm marrying Michelle," said Michael. "Head Elder gets what he wants. Nothing gets in his way. Do you realize the danger you've put Tony in?"

"Cut it out, Mike." George stepped between them, took his wife by the arm and dragged her to the other side of the room.

They spoke in heated, hissing whispers for a few moments. I had a good idea of what was being said. Sylvia's family handled the clan's finances and were prone to smother the slightest whiff of scandal. Her head dropped. She covered her mouth as if she was about to puke and rushed out of the room, slamming the door behind her.

George turned to our brother. They're not identical, but right then they seemed the mirror image of each other. "I'll handle her, but I want two things in return. First, a real DNA test so we know who Tony's real father is."

Mike nodded.

"Second, in exchange for my silence, I want the Wisdom Pearl."

I gasped through the stunned silence and barged between them, breaking the mirror illusion. "No. My mother died because you wanted the Wisdom Pearl. I don't care what anyone finds out. You're not getting it."

"Cat." Mike laid a gentle hand on my shoulder and pushed

me away. Then he cocked his head just like Dad did when facing down an enemy. "Or what? You'll go to Head Elder and tell him everything? Be my guest. That won't change a fucking thing. Sylvia and her son will be banished or killed. You'll lose face and wear a green hat." George's eyes flared at this expression, meaning the husband of a cheating wife. "I'll still be the Dragon Son. Head Elder might discipline me, but that's about it. You choose."

They stared at each for a long hateful moment. They were twins, but they'd never been brothers.

"Someday," George said, "You'll wish you'd given it to me. We could've been a great team, Mike. Taken back the power of the clan from Head Elder. I don't even care you slept with that bitch. It's her family that matters, not her. With their wealth and those pearls, nothing can stop us. We can take our clan to new heights. Last chance."

Mike slowly shook his head.

George strode out of the room, closing the door softly behind him.

Mike turned to me and Roy. I steeled myself because I knew what's coming. "You both must now swear on your honor not to share anything said in this room today, even if…" He took a hard breath. "Especially if Tony turns out to be my son."

Roy swore without hesitation. Of course he did. Mike was his best friend, his loyal brother, and he'd do anything to protect him, putting him first above everything, including the truth. Including me. How could I have thought, hoped, dreamed for the shreds of love between us? I swore my oath and left the room. All I wanted was for the wedding to be over so I could return to San Francisco and my life outside that web of lies.

Lennon

Roy stares at the floor, arms folded, and head bowed. Cat gazes out the bay windows, into the painful past that once separated them. I can feel the knot of tension. One false move and the fragile cord holding them together will snap.

His head lifts and turns toward her like a flower to the sun. He reaches out, laying his open palm in the space between them on the table. "You're right. Mike was the Dragon Son and I put my loyalty to him above everything, including my love for you. In reality, it was my honor I put first. I wanted nothing to damage it." He gives a humorless laugh. "Not even the truth. And what did that say about my honor, except that it was a damaged and frail thing? I paid the price. I lost you, the only woman I ever loved. I'm sorry."

Auntie Cat's cheeks redden as her eyes fill with tears. After a long, shaky breath, she takes his hand.

It's weird how I can feel happy after such an awful story, but I am glad. Dad forced their loyalty and their silence tore them apart. Now they're together again, I won't do or say anything that could ruin that. I wish I could leave and give them this moment, but I can't. There's no time.

"Could Dad have given Uncle George the Wisdom Pearl after all?" I ask. "I mean, in exchange for making Tony his heir?"

She nods. "Nothing else can explain George's new ability to manipulate people. Mike must have given him the combination to the safe in London and George repaid him by betraying him to Head Elder."

"That makes sense, but one thing's bothering me. Uncle George was banished for snooping in the caverns before Dad tried making Tony his heir. What was he doing there if he didn't already have the pearl?"

"That bothers me, too," says Roy. "I mean, maybe he and Mike had been making plans for longer than we know, and George went into the caverns to learn to use the pearl before he got his hands on it." He pauses, mulls, and shakes his head. "I can't believe Mike gave George the Wisdom Pearl, not for any reason."

"But he did." Cat's eyes cloud with disappointment. "Even though he swore to me he never would."

Did he? Since Dad's death, I've discovered how ruthless and selfish he could be, but nothing I've heard convinces me he'd give his brother that kind of power. Both the Wisdom and the Yin Pearl were recovered in London, but twenty years apart. Are they connected somehow? If the clan wasn't in such turmoil, I could call the London *kongsi* and ask for details, like when my father and uncle had been there. Since I don't know who to trust, a call like that could alert Uncle George that we're on to him.

I need to think like a leader and prioritize. I calculate a list in my head

1. Runaway (again)
2. Marry Penny (Vegas Baby!)
3. Fly to London
4. Heal Matthew

5. Reclaim the Yin Pearl

6. And…?

There's a lot of and. Should I delegate that to Tony or… I glance at Cat and Roy's sad, careworn faces. They need something useful to do besides sitting here, feeling guilty and wringing their hands. I can give them that and keep them busy while I sneak away.

I stand because it gives me more authority, but it feels weird because they're basically my second parents. I owe them a lot, including my life. I'm not going to be like Dad and dump on them and use them. I don't want to lie to them, either. Is withholding the truth any better? They'd know all about that.

"I need you guys to go to Tony and tell him everything you just told me. We have to assume Uncle George has the Wisdom Pearl, so we need to start planning a strategy around that."

Auntie Cat's eyes narrow because she knows me too well. "Aren't you coming with us?"

"No, not today. I can't."

"Why not?"

I don't want to tell her I'm supposed meet Penny at the art studio in half an hour. I change the subject with my one remaining question. "You said that when you were in the ancestral hall, you sensed the presence of Jade Dragon in the South China Sea. How were you able to do that?"

She and Roy exchange a look that tells me this is something else they've been honor bound to keep secret. She gives her head a little shake before turning to me with resolute eyes.

"It's a long story. After my mother died, my father became disgusted with his sons. He gave me the Yang Pearl and told me to be the Dragon Daughter. Ever since I wore it, I've been able to sense the presence of Jade Dragon."

Wow. No wonder she kept that secret. Talk about forbidden, though my grandfather liked breaking the rules. "Did you give it back to him?"

"No. Mike took it from me."

Of course he did, which was a damn shame. Why shouldn't there be a Dragon Daughter? I want to know all about it, but I don't have time. My phone buzzes and I look at the screen, thinking it's a message from Penny.

It's not. It's Jeremiah.

> Kid. We need to talk. Be at the Abode at 3 o'clock.

> Dude. Thanks for the short notice. Too bad I'm busy.

> Excuses are like assholes, everyone's got one. What's yours?

I send a gif of Cookie Monster watching a bouncing ball, captioned with "Me Very Very Busy." Then I turn off my phone and shove it in my pocket because I don't want to see his reply. I shouldn't be so disrespectful toward the new Head of the Crossroads, but I don't have time to watch him pound his chest at me. Whatever he wants can wait.

"Who was that?" asks Auntie Cat.

I sigh. "Jeremiah Walks Long."

She exchanges worried glances with Roy. "Are you in trouble?"

When am I not?

Penny

"You're too late," says Mona, the head welder of Junkyard Metallurgy. "I gave a guest lecture at San Francisco Art Institute yesterday and afterward a bunch of students asked to volunteer. More than we need. I had to turn people away. Sorry, but you're out of luck."

Story of our lives. Lennon and I have no luck, not unless we make it ourselves.

He shrugs as he says, "Thanks anyway."

I wrap my hand around his wrist to keep him from walking away. As a Strowler, I was born for moments like this. Charm is like smoke. I inhale the Bleater's need for affirmation and breathe out what they want to hear.

"What a hassle. You're the volunteer coordinator on top of everything else?"

"Yeah." Mona tugs at the gray wisps of hair stuck in her safety goggles. "I feel like I'm doing everything myself."

"That's why we want to volunteer. We saw how busy you are. Are you sure there's nothing we can do to help?"

Her eyes narrow. "You don't just want free entrance to Monstrosity?"

She's a nobody's fool. I need to be careful how thick I pour it on. I shake my head, my eyes big and solemn. "We've watched you guys build Doris for months. She's an amazing piece of art and we want to see her in action." I can see her eyes go fuzzy. Just a nudge more, one that soothes and coaxes. "There must be something we can do. A couple more volunteers could make a big difference."

Mona flutters her eyelashes. "Well, I suppose we could use more help." Her brow creases as if she's surprised by her own words. The no-nonsense look returns to her face. "We're starting our practice run at three this afternoon. Come back then. If anyone doesn't show up, you're in."

"We'll be here."

"All right, then." Mona frowns, rubbing her forehead as she walks away.

I take a deep breath and close my eyes as I exhale. She's a tough nut to crack.

"Was that Charm?" whispers Lennon.

"Yeah. I'll work on her more when we get back. Don't worry. We'll get in."

"Cool." He grins. "Can you teach me that?"

"No. Charm isn't a teachable skill. Strowlers are born with. It comes from," I frown as I press my fingers to my sternum, "somewhere in here. It's hard to explain. It's a part of us and we learn to use it as we grow older."

He nods along with a quizzical frown but doesn't reply.

"Want to go Banh Jovi for *cafe su da*?"

He nods again and stays in silent mode as we head outside. I used to believe that meant he was angry or sulking, but now I know he's just thinking. My thoughtful owl boy. He'll talk when he's ready, and he does, while we're waiting for our coffee.

"Most practitioners of *chi* skills believe the center of our energy is the *dantian*." He presses his fingers below his midsection. "But the Two Dragon Clan believes the power we got from Jade Dragon originates here." He presses his sternum in the same spot I pressed mine. "And spreads to our *dantian*."

"Interesting, how you got your powers from your dragon and we got ours from our fairy."

"Didn't Master Stoorworm give Strowlers anything besides guile?"

"Not really. I mean, dragons are hoarders, yeah? They don't give. Except your dragon and his pearls. I guess he's unusual."

That quiets him again. We take our coffee to the end of the pier and sit with our legs dangling over the side. There's a light wind blowing, and sunlight dapples the slow, lazy waves of the bay. Out toward the ocean, though, I can see the dark clouds of an oncoming storm.

"Asian dragons are different. They don't hoard," Lennon says before sipping his coffee.

"I didn't know that. I know they don't have wings and they're not considered evil. Though not all Europeans think dragons are evil. We don't. Strowlers, I mean. We see them more like a fertility symbol. I know that sounds kinda weird, but we do." I pause and take a sweet sip of *cafe su da* to ease the pain of my next words. "We also believe that dreaming of Master Stoorworm is bad luck. I dreamed about him a lot after Gerry died."

Lennon listens with owlish intensity before asking, "Have you dreamed of him recently?"

I shake my head. "I hope I never dream of him again."

After we eat, Lennon glances at his watch. "It's almost three."

"Nice watch. Is it new?"

He nods. "Birthday gift from Tony."

I could have guessed that. "Do you like it?"

"No."

But he's wearing it anyway because that's what he and Tony do. Wind each other up.

We go back inside the warehouse and the ground floor is crawling with activity. Artists and makers are tinkering with the giant spider while a burlesque dance troupe called Fishnet Fatale are warming up in the common area. We join the volunteers gathered around the stairs. Most are college-aged and chattering amongst themselves.

Mona stands above us and taps a wrench on the metal rail to get our attention. Everyone quiets down, and she details the volunteer duties. I try paying attention, but I keep getting distracted by the dancers going through their routine.

When was the last time I danced?

About two months ago, but it seems like forever. My old life was far from perfect, but I miss it. Dancing and designing clothing is all I ever wanted to do. I've put those things on hold to heal Matthew and help Lennon, but I won't give them up forever. When this is over, I want my life back.

But what if that's not possible?

My heart pounds. People behind me are hissing and it takes me a moment to realize they're whispering. Then they giggle, as if there's something funny going on, but there's nothing funny about me losing my life. I suck in my breath as Mona strikes the metal rail hard. My ears ring and my head clears.

She scowls before she speaks. "This is a complex operation. If you can't follow explicit instructions, you need to leave right now."

And I need to get my head back in the game. I turn and size up the couple standing behind me. Neither are dressed for greasy, hard work and the woman has nice nails, making her my mark. I tap into that fairy energy, allowing it to make my expression a mirror to hers. Our eyes meet. I shake my head.

She shakes hers, too.

"There's got to be a better way to get into Monstrosity," I whisper.

She blinks before saying, "I know, right?" She tugs on her boyfriend's hand. Moments later, they drift away.

I wink at Lennon. He looks impressed, but he shouldn't be. She was a much easier mark than Mona.

After her speech, Mona does a headcount, glances over at us and give a thumbs up. Lennon and I fist-bump on the down-low.

Hours pass as we learn to dismantle and reassemble Doris and her web, including two full-run music rehearsals with Fishnet Fatale. Finally, Mona tells everyone it's a wrap, but to stick around so Junkyard Metallurgy can thank us for all our hard work. The DJ starts playing dance music while a cooler full of beer is cracked open.

Lennon and I look at his fancy watch. It's half past eight. "Do you want to hang?" he asks.

I almost say no until I see the boxes of pizza being delivered. My mouth waters. "Yes."

We each grab a beer and some pizza. Then we head over to the staircase, climb a few steps, and settle down.

"Think we'll get in trouble?" asks Lennon.

I hold up my bottle. "The legal drinking age in London is 18."

"Same in Hong Kong."

We share a grin before we clink and drink and discover that pepperoni pizza tastes fantastic with beer. While we eat, I look out at the party, at people talking, laughing, drinking, and dancing. A déjà vu feeling shivers through me. "What does this remind you of?"

He answers without hesitation. "The first time we met at the Beggars Banquet."

Where we hid the on stairs, ate, and talked, and shared our first kiss. Our eyes meet and there's no question we want to relive that moment. Our mouths touch, sweet and soft, like our first time, except now we taste of beer and pizza instead of tea and sweets. I guess we are growing up.

Lennon sighs and rests his chin on his knee. "I like it here. It's the only place where I feel like myself, but after we get the pearls, I don't think I'll be able to come back."

"You don't know that." Even as I say those words, I know better. He's right. There's no way he can be both the Dragon Son and an edgy street artist. I want to change that, but I don't know how and don't want to think about it right now.

I pull out my phone and check the screen. No messages yet, so I send one to Bridie.

> At the studio. Everything going as planned.
> Lots to do. I'm spending the night here.
> Trust me.

I turn to Lennon. "Take out your phone." He does and stares at the screen with a puzzled frown. Uh-oh. "What's wrong?"

"Nothing. I mean, there should be something. I guess. Jeremiah sent me a text and I sassed him back. I thought he would've replied by now, but no."

"How did you sass him?"

He shows me a gif of Cookie Monster watching a bouncing ball.

I snicker. "Epic. What do you think he wants?"

"Dunno. To watch him piss all over the Crossroads so I know it's his?"

My snicker becomes a laugh. "That can wait." I hold up my phone and tap the night mode icon. Then I nod for him to do the same. "It can all wait until tomorrow. If this is our last night here, then let's enjoy it."

His smile lights up his solemn face. We get up and head downstairs to the makeshift dance floor in the middle of warehouse. The DJ is spinning a dance remix of Lady Gaga's Telephone. Talk about the perfect song. We shout out the "stop calling" chorus with everyone else and mimic hanging up a phone, even though I've never done such a thing.

The first time I asked Lennon to dance, he said he didn't know how. Now, he's dancing in decent time to the beat, graceful as a martial artist should be. I have this feeling he's been practicing, waiting for the chance to dance with me again. I almost want to ask, but I don't because it will ruin the moment.

The music mixes and transitions to Shallow. My feet falter. We stand in the middle of the floor as other couples twine together, moving slowly and sensuously to the music. Strowlers only permit married couples to slow dance. If a single couple slow dances, it's the same as announcing their engagement. Lennon shrugs as if to say, I will if you will. We're getting married, so I will. With a nervous giggle, I wrap my arms around his shoulders. His arms move around my waist and we shift awkwardly from foot-to-foot before we find each other's rhythm. It doesn't feel like real dancing, but it's nice. Sexy. His body feels good moving against mine.

I close my eyes and listen to the lyrics. The song's couple sound so much like us, in the deep end, so far from shallow water, we can't see the bottom. Lennon's forehead presses against mine as if to tell me he's listening, too, and agrees. Our lips touch and part, and we kiss as if we're the only people there.

Until a voice says, "Aw, they're so cute."

My eyes pop open. Two of the Fishnet Fatale dancers are beside us. They're an interracial couple, too, Black and Asian. One of women winks while the other blows us a kiss before they sway away. We both turn bright red, but I'm not sorry. It feels good being able to kiss in public and be cute instead of a disgrace.

The night goes on like that, eating, drinking, and dancing. Being normal, I guess. I mean, the people here are a bunch of artsy weirdos like us. This is so much like the life I imagined for myself, I don't want it to end. But in the words of Prince, "Parties aren't meant to last" and as this one winds down, Lennon and I stagger into his studio.

We've only had two beers, so neither of us is drunk. Maybe buzzed? I'd probably feel better if I didn't have indigestion from dancing on a full stomach. We roll onto the cot, clasp hands, and stare at the ceiling.

"That was great," Lennon says with a sigh.

"Yeah." I close my eyes. Best night of my life? Not really, but close. I'm about to say so but fall asleep instead.

Lennon

I groan, pressing my palm to my forehead. "Is this a hangover?"

"Dunno. I've never had one before." Penny sits up and kneads her temples. "Do you feel like you need to puke?"

"No. You?"

"No. Maybe it's just a wee hangover. I feel like I need coffee more than anything."

"Coffee. Yes." I groan again as I sit up beside her. My mouth tastes gross, like dry old beer. We're wearing the same clothes we worked and sweated in all day yesterday. I probably look like a hobo, but she somehow manages to look amazing, even with her makeup smeared all over her eyes. This is the second time I've woken up with her in the same bed. I like it. I want her there every morning.

She looks up at the skylight. The cloudy sky is keeping the studio dark and cold. "What time is it?"

I check my Tony watch. "Almost nine."

"Oh man. We're probably so busted by, like, everyone."

I shrug. "I don't care."

Her smile is like sunshine breaking through those clouds. "Me, neither. Coffee and then phones, yeah?"

"Sounds like a plan."

We head for the bathrooms to wash up and change. Both bathrooms are gender neutral and one has a shower stall and one doesn't. When Penny and I are married, we can take showers together. That thought does things to me and I hurry into the shower-less bathroom before she notices.

I'm done first and I wait in the hall, forcing myself not to look at my phone. It would only ruin what's left of our morning. Then Penny steps out of the bathroom with damp hair, no makeup, and wearing a pair of leggings and T-shirt she'd spray painted with cool, abstract designs. She looks like a Matisse painting and I fall in love with her again.

Her eyes narrow. "You okay?"

I nod because I can't speak. There's too much I want to say.

We hold hands as we walk along the Embarcadero toward the Ferry Building. A cold wind blows off the bay and we move closer, arms around each other's waist to stay warm. I like how this feels. It can't end just because other people say so. I'm not giving up Penny. If Tony doesn't like it, too bad. He can take the pearls and be the Dragon Son or shut up about it.

The Ferry Building is a huge, historic warehouse with a clock tower at the end of Market Street. It's now a tourist trap full of specialty shops and restaurants, making it the perfect place for us to sit and scheme since no one we know would ever come in here. We settle in the corner of a trendy café with our lattes and croissants and take a few bites and sips before turning on our phones.

Penny winces as she studies her screen. "Bridie's having a fit, as predicted." She starts tapping out a message.

My screen is empty. Nothing from Tony, or Auntie Cat, or anyone. Either they're waiting for my next move or they're going ahead without me because they think I'm incompetent. Either works for me.

We set down our phones and pick up our cups. Time to implement Phase Two.

"Okay, I'll take you home and then I'll…" I stop talking because both our phones are buzzing. I pick mine up and look at the message from Jeremiah.

Get your punk ass to the Abode right now.

Penny holds up her screen so I can see it.

I know you're with Lennon. I want you both to come to the Abode right now.

She glances at my screen. "Nice."

"He likes you more than he likes me."

"You mean he likes my mother." She grimaces. "What do we do? Ignore him?"

I think about it for a second. "If we do, it'll look suspicious. Let's go there and let him yell at us and get it over with."

"Sounds fun."

Hell, yeah.

We head back to the Kinetic Collective to get my scooter. It's noon and traffic is heavy along the Embarcadero, so it's taking longer than usual to get to Bayview, but I'm okay with that. Penny's arms feel good around my waist. I wish we could keep driving, out of the city and to wherever.

We make it to the Beggar Clan's compound and drive in like usual, no biggie, no one stops us. When we reach the entrance to the Abode, two brawny, camo-clad dudes come striding forward. The taller one holds out his palm while the shorter one announces, "You must submit to a pat-down before you can proceed."

Penny and I exchange wide-eyed glances. She scoffs. "You're not laying your manky hands on me."

Tall nods toward me. "Not you. Just him."

Jeremiah really wants to break my balls. Ordinarily, I wouldn't care, except to say something snarky, like 'Aren't you gonna kiss me first?' But now, I don't want them finding the Yang Pearl. "Tell your chief that if he doesn't trust me, we're not meeting."

They don't like that. I can see it in their steroidal frowns. They step aside to confer with their shoulder mics before waving me through. We saunter past their glares and enter the Abode where our escorts await. We're led along the edge of the building because the mats are down and the Beggars are working out, either exercising or sparring, which is odd. Noon is prime begging time when they scour the city for information without being noticed behind their filthy rags and pathetic cardboard signs. Inside the fight cage, a man and a woman use knives to slash at each other with vicious intensity while their coaches holler instructions from the sidelines. Maybe Jeremiah ordered extra training now that the Beggars are head clan of the Crossroads.

When we reach the far end of the Abode, Jeremiah comes marching out of the corner office, clutching the staff of the Beggar Chief. He's wearing camouflage pants and a sleeveless black undershirt that rocks his bulging muscles, burn scars, and tribal tattoos. If John Walks Long was alive, we wouldn't be here right now engaging in useless bullshit. Penny's mind brushes mine. I let her in.

What a nob she says.

Which is kind of strange because she didn't used to dislike him that I know of, not until recently.

I must have thought that aloud because she answers, *He's got the hots for Bridie.* She pauses and I feel the tension rise within her. *And Uncle Christy would gladly give her to him.*

But Jeremiah isn't a Strowler.

Yeah, but Bridie's already disgraced herself several times over. Her marrying into the Beggar Clan, the actual head of the Crossroads no less, would be a golden feather in Uncle Christy's cap. I'm getting a bad feeling about this.

Jeremiah takes a seat in the high-backed, patched and frayed armchair that serves as the Beggar Chief's throne. He waves away our guards before beckoning us to join him.

We exchange looks. Time to turbo-charge our teen attitude. We both sigh like it's a huge effort and approach as if he's the Vice-Principal and we got caught skipping class. He stares at us with slate-gray eyes, waiting.

Penny heaves another sigh before saying, "Walk in peace, Beggar Chief."

I go for broke with, "Sup, dude?"

"I don't have time for little pissants like you," his gravel voice grates out. "You're a disgrace to your clans and your families." A cocky smile forms on my lips, but his next words slap it right off. "The entire Crossroads is in chaos and people are dying while you two play games."

"Who's dying?" I ask.

"The Beggar Clan and the Shinobi are at war. They assassinated one of my men last night. It's worse in Japan. They've killed more than a dozen Beggars. Tensions were high after Hasaki killed my father, but everything exploded when I became head of the Crossroads."

My strategy worked. I threw our fight so he would win and have to deal with the consequences. In the back of my mind, I knew there would be a body count, but still, my stomach twists. Is it my fault people are dead? Maybe, but it's his, too. He wanted to be the Big Cheese, and it's on him if his people are dying.

I also can't help thinking how this works to my advantage.

If the Shinobi are busy with their vendetta against the Beggar Clan, they won't go after me.

Jeremiah realizes this, too, from the glare he fixes on me. "You two have fun last night?"

I go back into surly teen mode and shrug. "Yeah."

Penny does the same. "Yeah."

"Yeah." He pulls out his phone and turns the screen toward us. On it is a photo of me and her kissing while we slow danced. "Penny, what do you think your uncle will say when he sees this?"

Bastard! He's been playing me and it's my fault for underestimating him.

Penny's arms fold tight. "You've been spying on us. Why? To blackmail us?"

Jeremiah shakes his head. "Not at all. Your uncle asked me to keep an eye on you and report back on anything…" He pauses and thinks. "Untoward is the word he used. But there's enough chaos on the Crossroads. I don't need the Two Dragon Clan and the Strowlers going at it, especially since we're supporting his ass," he juts his chin at me, "as Dragon Son." He shoves his phone back his pocket. "You two behave from now on and no one else will see that photo."

"What do you mean, behave?" I ask.

He smirks, which is weird because he's not a smirky guy. He flicks on his shoulder mic and says, "Now."

The corner office door opens, and two red-headed men stride out dressed in boots, jeans, plaid shirts and colorful neck scarves. I only met them once in passing, but I recognize them as Christy Sparrow's two oldest sons, Jack and Brendan. By instinct, I put myself between Penny and them, but she nudges past me to meet them halfway.

Her hands go to her hips as she speaks, "What the devil are you two doing here?"

"Come to fetch you, girl," says Jack. "Your romping days are over. You're coming home to stay."

"What do you mean, home? The Nest?"

"Of course. Da's orders."

"Tell Uncle Christy I'm an adult on the Wayward Way and he can't give me orders, which he full knows."

"Yer mum and brother are already there," says Brendan. "Snug in a caravan, safe and sound, as you soon will be, too."

Penny hesitates at the mention of her family. She takes a tight breath. "What do you mean?"

"I mean Da's the Upright Man and he knows what's best for the family."

"I'm not going with you."

Jack waves a dismissive hand. "You're coming back to the fold, Penny Sparrow, and that's the end of it." Her cousins come up on either side of her take hold of her arms. "You can walk out or carried out, your choice."

I surge forward, but Jeremiah blocks me with this staff. "Stay in your lane, kid. This is their clan's business. They're here with my permission. If you take on them, you take on me and the entire Beggar Clan."

That all sounds like a great idea, especially since I'm halfway to gathering enough *chi* to blow him against the wall. And then what? Penny and I will run to the airport, fly to London, heal Matthew, and keep running because everyone will be after us. Still sounds like a good idea. I lift my hand.

Penny's mind touches mine. *Don't. We need to be canny about this.*

Canny? I know she used a Strowler phrase to distract me and it works. I lower my hand.

Clever. I'll call you. We'll figure this out.

Jack strides up so we're standing chest to chest. He's maybe an inch taller than me and he uses that to look down on me as best he can. "Listen, ye little shite. You stay away from my cousin, yeah?"

Cousin. Juliet had a cousin, Tybalt, who Romeo killed in a duel which made everything much worse for them. My heart pounds as my *chi* energy drains away.

My silence infuriates him. He pokes my chest. "I challenge you. Name the day."

Well, shit. He's as determined to fight me as Tybalt was Romeo. What's the clever answer to this? Then it hits me, and I almost smile. "Here. Noon. November 1."

When Penny and I will be long gone. Yeah, I'm throwing another fight and will be branded a coward, again, but it'll be so worth it.

Jack looks at Jeremiah, who nods his consent.

Well done, says Penny. I feel her pleasure even though her expression doesn't change.

Her cousins tug at her and she walks along without further struggle. It's like torture, being separated when we need each other the most. She looks over her shoulder at me and our eyes lock. We'll never truly be separated, not as long as we share the Silent Speech.

Jeremiah raises his staff to my chest and doesn't lower it until Penny and her cousins leave the Abode. "Okay, kid, we're done here."

"You're a dick," I spit out.

"Yeah, I am. You need to learn to be one, too."

I scowl like I'm angry and confused, but I'm thinking, Halloween. You'll find out how much of dick I can be then.

Penny

History repeats itself as I'm once again snapped up and taken to the Nest against my will. Last time this happened, I was facing Kingfisher and his evil intentions. The time, I'm facing Uncle Christy and his best intentions. Right now, I'm seeing little difference between the two. Both act the bully and dismiss the rights of women and children. I'm seated between my cousins in the back of an SUV. No one says anything as we take the bumpy back roads, passing warehouses, rusty piers, and construction projects abandoned during the last economic crisis. I seethe and strive against a desire to struggle for struggle's sake, but I don't because I need to take my own advice and be canny.

Wind whips at our car as dark clouds gather overhead. It's raining by the time we get to the Nest which matches my stormy mood. The SUV pulls up in front of a caravan that's parked beside Uncle Christy's house. It looks brand new, but I'm not in any mood to appreciate that as I step inside, mad as a wet hen. Bridie is sitting the kitchen table, chewing her thumbnail, while Kai slumps on the couch, pecking away at his phone.

My brother speaks first, his hazel eyes dark with anger. "She pulled me out of school. Says we have to live here now. It's not fair."

Bridie remains silent. Her eyes are red from weeping.

I sit across from her. "What's that mean, live here? From now on? What about our apartment and your job?"

She clears her throat, but her voice still crackles. "I quit. Told management we'd be out by the end of the week."

My mouth drops open. No. Not again. Her weakness, her inability to cope with life will ruin everything. I take a breath and outrage pours out. "How could you? What about us? Kai and school? Me and my business? I have customers and clothes to make."

"This is a nice big caravan. We can make room for…"

I slam my hand on the table. "What about money? How are we going to make a living? Or did you think about that?" Tears trickle down her face as I rant. Her lips press into a thin line of misery to hold back her sobs. I feel like a monster so I stop and huff. Then I whisper, "What about Matthew?"

The front door swings open without a knock and Uncle Christy steps inside. He eyes me with sharp disapproval. "I can hear you from outside, girl. Don't be talking to your mam that way. It's disrespectful."

I stand and face him, hands on hips. "What about you, snapping me at the Abode? That's disrespectful."

"It's all the respect you deserve for acting the romp. You put your family in danger. Now, you're all here, safe, where you belong."

My arms fold tight. "What danger?"

"Will you listen to her?" He gestures at me with an incredulous hand. "What danger? You and your boyfriend swan around, playing your games, while the Crossroads is afire. The clans are at war, killing each other, and you think you can sit pretty with the boy who's causing it all."

He pauses as if expecting me to say something. I don't, but I'm thinking, well, that was our plan, me and Lennon, to look ignorant and naïve while we plotted our getaway. We didn't count on pissing off everyone so much that they'd act against us.

Uncle Christy huffs. "I put out the word, as did the other Upright Men and leaders of the Gypsy clans. We're not involved in this conflict. Our Nests and caravans are off limits and if any harm comes to any of us, there'll be a worldwide Gypsy vendetta against the perpetrator. The Two Dragon Clan, the Beggars, the Shinobi, they have enough on their plates fighting each other. They don't need us piling on. You stay here, you're safe. End of discussion."

I turn to Bridie. She won't look at me. I shout-whisper, "Mum. We can't stay here. What about… everything?"

Her voice shakes as she speaks. "I told Christy about Matthew."

"What? What did you tell him?"

"That he's alive, but in a coma, and his parents told us the Dragon Son can heal him, and that you would take Lennon to London so he can heal him."

She didn't tell him about the pearls. I breathe with relief despite my fury.

My uncle snorts. "I can't believe you swallowed that cock and bull story. And that boy let you swallow it so he could romp with Penny. What kind of mother are you, pimping your daughter to save your man?"

Bridie covers her eyes with her fingers. Tears seep through the cracks. Her shoulders shake as she speaks in a husky whisper, "You're right. Matty would never save himself by putting Penny's virtue at risk or her life in danger. And he'd never forgive me for putting her in this position. We're stashing this game. It's over."

There's a silence, as if dropping a brick into a deep well and waiting for it to hit bottom. The splash is like an explosion.

"No," shouts Kai, tears filling his eyes. "I want my dad back!"

I suck in a breath so I don't shout. "She can't speak for me. I'm an adult, on the Wayward Way, and I'll do as I see fit."

Christy shakes his head. "I can speak for you, girl. I'm the Upright Man and the head of this family here in the States, and you'll do as I say, like it or no."

Canny. I have to be canny and throw this back on him to deflect off me. "I know why you're doing this. You don't care if Matthew lives or dies. You want Bridie to marry Jeremiah Walks Long."

Another stunned silence fills the caravan. Even Bridie stops crying and stares from me to her brother with startled eyes.

"What?" His brow beetles. "Where did you hear such nonsense?"

"Why else would Jeremiah help you grab me if not to get to Bridie?"

"Is that true?" demands Kai.

Christy addresses him rather than me. "Fact is, your mother's done. No decent Strowler will have her. First, she married a molly. No surprise he wasn't man enough for her. Then she had herself a Westminster Wedding with Matthew." He holds up his hand at our sounds of outrage. Molly is a derogatory word for a gay man, while Westminster Wedding is a term for a marriage between a Strowler and a member of another Crossroads clan, but it also means the marriage of a rogue to a whore. "I call like it is. Then she took up with Bleater Bill and nearly disgraced herself with Kingfisher. After all that, you think I'd stand in Jeremiah's way if he wants to court her?"

"No one is courting me. Not Jeremiah or anyone," protests Bridie. "Not while Matthew is still alive."

"He's in a coma and the Dragon Son can't miraculously heal him. I can't believe you're such a gom, Bridie." He scoffs. "I swear, I'd go put a bullet in that Lennon's head right now if it hadn't been Matthew's parents who told you that story."

"Why would they tell us that if it's not true?" I demand.

"Because they're desperate, and desperate people will grasp at any straw offered them, just like your mother. Did Lennon tell you he can cure Matthew?"

I can't give away too much. I stammer so I can stall while I think. "Well, not exactly. He, um, he said his father died before teaching him everything, but he's willing to try, and hopes Matthew's parents can tell him what to do."

"See? That's how the Two Dragon Clan stayed on top for so long, making everyone believe they have magical powers."

"You know how powerful the Dragon Son is."

"Smoke and mirrors as far as I'm concerned, until I see different."

"You saw different at the *kongsi* when the front door blew open."

"Smoke and mirrors."

Arguing is pointless. Uncle Christy has made up his mind. I turn away and head for the back of the caravan.

"Where are you going?" he asks.

"The loo."

He holds out his hand. "Give me your phone."

"What?" Shit.

"Your phone. Give it up, girl, or I'll take it and you don't want that."

I dig into my pocket and place it on the counter because I don't want to hand him anything.

He turns to Kai. "Yours, too, son."

My brother clutches his phone to his chest. "What? Why?"

"I know full well you and your sister are thick as thieves.

There'll be no contacting the outside world for the duration." He snatches away Kai's phone and says to Bridie, "Yours too, love."

Her watery green eyes widen. "But… I need it… I… I need to call my students… their parents. Tell them their lessons are cancelled." Even through these weak protests, she digs through her purse and fishes out her phone.

I'm having such a hard time not hating her right now.

"You can come to house and make your calls while Joanne or I watch."

She gives a meek nod, her head hung low.

"Good. Now, the cupboards are well stocked and the tellies have all the best channels. Settle yourselves down and relax. It's over. The sooner you face it, the better for us all."

He takes our silence as his cue to leave, closing the door with a soft click.

Kai and I turn to our mother, mouths open. She lifts her head and presses a finger to her lips, her gaze sharp and determined.

My brother and I look at each other, dumbfounded. Then I mouth to Bridie, "You were shamming?"

She nods and wipes her still-running eyes before standing and motioning us to follow. My anger takes flight. She's not a coward. I can be proud of her. Whatever comes next, this means everything.

We creep into the back bedroom and Bridie closes the door behind us. Then she opens her suitcase, digs out her Tampon box, and pulls out her work phone.

I smack my forehead. I'd forgotten about it. "But, won't they cut it off since you quit?"

"I didn't quit. I poured out a full dose of Charm and convinced them I needed another week off for the family emergency."

I turn to Kai. We're both smiling so wide, you'd think our faces will split. There's only one problem. "I don't know Lennon's number by heart. Do you know Aaron's?"

He shakes his head as both our grins disappear. "Uncle Christy wouldn't let me bring our computers."

I rub my forehead. So, how do I get a hold of Lennon? I only use social media for my business and he doesn't use it at all. I don't even think he has an email address. There's got to be a way.

Kai snaps his fingers. "Cinch!"

"Cinch?" asks Bridie.

"It's an online game platform, and it has a DM feature." He shakes his head at our mother's confusion and holds out his hand. "Give me the phone." We watch while he downloads the Cinch app. "Aaron and I message each other here all the time. Mostly about game stuff. It goes to his phone like a regular message."

Bridie reaches for my hand and we both squeeze tight as we watch him log into the app and open the message screen. Kai's handle is SliceNdice. Aaron's is ThrillKillah.

911

Sup?

Need your phone #

What happened?

Tell you in a minute give me your # and
Lennon's too.

Bridie takes a deep, shaky breath. "Are you scared?"

"I don't have time to be scared," I reply.

"Matty really won't forgive me for sacrificing you."

"Mum. This isn't about sacrifice. I'm a warrior on the Crossroads and this is what we do. We fight with whatever we've got."

I've got Lennon, and he's got me, and we're going to fight together, win or lose… no. Win. We can only win because losing isn't an option. What it will take to win…

That's the scary part.

Penny

I'm in the bathroom, smearing on a quick layer of makeup, when I feel him. A touch on my shoulder, a caress on my cheek, a whisper in my ear.

Penny.

I shiver as goosebumps pebble my skin, but I don't shriek. I also whisper.

Da?

It's Samhain, when spirits walk the earth, but I've never felt Gerry's presence before. Had it taken all these years for his soul to cross an ocean and a continent to reach us? Tears fill my eyes. I'd hoped he'd passed on, even knowing full well he couldn't. After he died, his oldest brother, Oren, got possession of his body. As punishment for his "sins," Oren buried him on the Crossroads, dooming him to wander forever.

You're on the dub tonight, yeah? he asks.

Yeah. Any advice?

Use your wits. You're every bit the wide boy I was.

My throat tightens as tears fill my eyes. I know I'm imagining this, but I still panic when I feel him drawing away.

Where are you going? Please stay. Or at least see Bridie and Kai before you leave.

Before the night is over, I will. Godspeed, Penny Lane. The only ones who ever used my middle name were my fathers. I inhale through my nose to keep my tears from falling. Ghost fingers touch my cheek as his presence fades away.

Someone pounds on the door. I almost jump out of my skin.

"You gonna be in there forever?" demands Kai.

"Piss off," I call out as I wipe my eyes.

"I'll have to piss outside if you don't leg it."

I take a deep breath before opening the door and brushing past him. I take a moment, and a few breaths, before joining Bridie in the kitchen. Like me, she and Kai are also dressed in all black. We had a vague idea of splitting up and sending Christy and his men on a wild goose chase, trying to catch us.

I hear Gerry's whisper *You need a better game than that.*

He's right. I think for a moment. "Is there any way we can get costumes?"

Bridie frowns. "Why?"

"Because it's better to fit in than stand out, yeah?"

"True enough." She rubs her chin and gets that crafty gleam in her eyes, the one I've so missed for so long.

Kai steps out of the loo and eyes us. "What's up?"

"We're cutting a sham on your uncle."

He snorts. "About damn time."

He's damn right.

We're escorted by guards to Uncle Christy's house. He's wearing a fine suit and colorful silk neck scarf, but is otherwise unadorned since fancy dress in beneath the dignity of an Upright Man. He stares on us with cutty-eyes. "What are you lot up to?"

I cross my arms, roll my eyes, and scowl like a sullen chit.

"Can I have my phone back?" asks Kai.

"No. Stop asking." His squint becomes less suspicious since we're behaving as expected.

It's up to Bridie to do the trick. She can't use Charm on a fellow Strowler, but she can wheedle. "Christy, this is hard enough. I could barely convince them to leave the caravan. How much fun do you think it will be for them without costumes? Perhaps Joanne can fix us up?"

"I don't want to wear some dumb costume," I say.

"I want my phone," says Kai.

Christy huffs. "If your mam wants you in fancy dress, you'll wear fancy dress." He calls over his shoulder, "Joanne, love, Bridie and her kinchin need Halloween duds."

Auntie Joanne pops out of the kitchen, dressed in green chiffon, glitter, lace, and wings, with a wee top hat, as if she were a leprechaun fairy. "I expected as much." Her delighted smile tweaks my conscious. I don't enjoy shamming the kind and good-hearted, but what choice do I have?

"Come in, come in." She herds us into the master bedroom where the king-size mattress is buried beneath a massive pile of costumes. She claims it's her duty as the Nest's Mother Bird to provide fancy dress for those in need, but I think she just enjoys shopping at the Halloween stores. "The lads will be along to cart this lot to the party, but since you're family, you have first pick."

"You're so kind," says Bridie with a thankful smile.

"I'll leave you to it. Shannon and I have to finish dipping the caramel apples."

After she closes the door behind her, we dig through the pile. Many of the costumes are pajama-style onesies that will easily fit over our clothes. Kai unfurls a skeleton onesie and hold it to his shoulders. I tug out a black cat onesie.

"The way you're dressed, you don't need that. You could just wear this." Bridie holds out a black cat mask.

I put on the mask and look at myself in the full-length door mirror. The mask covers most of my face, except my mouth and chin.

Think sharp, whispers Gerry.

I lick my lips, tasting the pale pink gloss. Then I turn to Bridie, with her ruby red lips. "Can I borrow your lipstick?"

We leave the bedroom in our fancy dress. Kai is wearing the skeleton with its white skull hood covering over his hair and forehead. Mum is dressed like a fairy godmother in glittery chiffon with wings and a wand. I go full spiv in a rainbow unicorn onesie, the hood pulled up so that the sparkling horn juts from my forehead. It's baggy enough to wear over my clothes and hide the cat mask tucked under my shirt.

Auntie Joanne clasps her hand to her chest at the sight of us. Uncle Christy harrumphs and barks orders. "Lads, take up the costumes and haul them to the gym. Ladies, we'll leave you to the food."

Bridie and I follow Joanne, her daughters- and daughters-in-law into the kitchen. Shannon, Jack's wife, starts handing me a plate of apples still steaming from being dunked in caramel.

"No, no." Joanne waves her away. "Penny can carry the barm brack." She hands me a tray of sweet loaves speckled with sultanas. Then she points to the end of one and winks. "You'll want to cut there."

Barm brack, a traditional Samhain treat, is cooked with a ring inside and whoever finds it is the next to be wed. If they only knew I'm about to fly to Las Vegas to do just that.

It's almost ten p.m. when we leave the house with Christy and Joanne. A bright crescent moon shines through the scattered clouds. The ground is damp from a previous downpour and we have to step carefully to avoid pothole puddles. Caravan doors pop open as we pass and people come streaming out to join us, including small children. Strowler parties start late and last into the next morning. When I was a child, I loved it. As an adult woman, I know that I'm now expected to serve all night and clean the next morning. Bugger that. I can't think of a better reason to walk the Wayward Way.

The gym has been transformed into a Halloween wonderland with orange and black streamers, strings of flickering pumpkin and ghost lights, and ghoulish, full-size cardboard cutouts of spiders, witches, monsters and the lot. We set the food on tables already laden with treats and drinks for both kids and adults. The exercise equipment has been pushed to the side to create a dance floor, and a DJ is set up in a corner, starting the party off with Monster Mash. Lights shine down on the bleachers since they're the best place to sit, but also because a fight will inevitably break out and Christy will order the combatants into the ring to finish it.

I glance around, taking in the locations of the doors and bathrooms. Timing is everything and I've got hours to go before I can scarper. A pink unicorn comes skipping up and links arms with me. It's my cousin, Fiona. She squees before shouting, "Unicorn power!"

Her cry is echoed by three more unicorns in various colored onesies already on the floor. With a reluctant smile, I allow her to tug me along. They're all about her age, fourteen, and I feel old as the hills as we join them. Their chatter is all about the Likely Lads lined up against the wall, drinking beer and eying us. Sixteen is considered marriageable age among Strowlers. Back in the day, they often contracted girls to marry boys they barely knew. Nowadays, Strowler youth meet and take a fancy to one another at weddings, funerals, and parties like this, but because their families' constantly travel, they're unlikely to see each more than a handful of times before they're wed.

The unicorn crew's squeals intensify when the DJ transitions to Disturbia by Rihanna. They start dancing and I join them because why not? It's an easy way to blend in. Others, mostly women and children, join us we gyrate to the beat and sing along. I glance around. Bridie is with Joanne, fussing over the food. Kai stands against the wall next to our cousin, Casey, who's wearing a Spiderman onesie. Christy is standing amidst a group of beer-guzzling men that includes his older sons, except he's sipping and keeping a discreet, close eye on everyone, including me, or rather, especially me from his look when our eyes meet.

I glance away to the line-up of Likely Lads and notice one eyeing me like he knows me. Maybe he's heard word I'm Christy's romping niece. If that's giving him any ideas, it'll be my pleasure to shoot them down. The song ends and I leave the dance floor since I'm already sweating from wearing two sets of clothes. I relieve Shannon from punchbowl duty so she can breastfeed. The lad approaches as I'm ladling out drinks. Here we go. I put on my sour bint face and give him the evil eye. He's on the shorter end of medium height, red-faced and muscular. The sort of lad who grows up learning manual labor and bare-knuckle boxing.

"Hi," he says, "I'm Cooper Sparrow."

"Oh, hi." My sour face dissolves into a smile. Strowlers don't intermarry with those of the same Nest name. It'd be like marrying your cousin. "I'm Penny Sparrow. I didn't know there were other Sparrows in the Nest."

"We got here last night."

"Well, it's nice to meet you." I hand him a cup of punch.

"Thanks. Same. You should come meet the fam."

"Sure. I'm busy now, but later. I'll bring my mother and brother."

"Great." He strolls away, sipping his punch.

I exhale. I need to stop being so suspicious. Sometimes a guy is just a guy. Still, I want to avoid any more encounters with Likely Lads, so I stay with the married women, distributing food and minding small children to give their mothers a break. I don't go to the ladies' room until I'm almost bursting because pulling down the onesie and my trousers isn't fun. I go to the end stall with the room's single window. It's too high and narrow for me to squeeze through, but the breeze cools me off. I almost want to spend the whole evening here, but Christy would notice my absence. The stench of cigarette smoke floating in seals the deal. I flush and as I shrug on and zip up the onesie, I hear male voices outside. One sounds like Christy. I'm not too interested until I feel a ghostly nudge. Gerry, urging me to eavesdrop. I stand on the toilet seat and listen.

"I'm warning you," says my uncle. "she's not just a romp. She's a wild one. You'll have to keep her sealed tight or she'll scarper."

"We'll be halfway up the Oregon coast by the time she comes to," says an American man. "There's a Sparrow Nest near Tillamook. We'll plant there until she calms down."

My heart pounds. I take a deep breath like Lennon taught me to calm my energy so I can hear better.

"Are you sure it's safe?" asks Christy.

"My wife knows her potions. Cooper's already had a nice chat with her. After the bonfire, he'll slip something in her drink and get her alone before she passes out." He pauses. "How wild you reckon she'll be?"

"Wild enough. She can fight."

"We'll keep her calm for the duration then."

"Those potions won't hurt her? Six months is a long time to be doped up."

"I told you, Mellie knows what she's doing. It's not dope. It's herbs. The kind Strowler women know."

"I need your word she'll be safe and returned to us unharmed."

"On my honor."

"You've got yourself a deal." There's a pause as I hear them spit and shake hands.

"What about the mother and brother?"

"I'll handle them."

They walk away, their footsteps crunching the gravel.

I step off the toilet and slide to the floor. I want to puke, scream, and pound the wall in that order. Then I cover my face because I also want to cry. My own uncle, the one I thought was half-way decent, is throwing me over the bridge. How could he? Stupid question. I know full well. I'm a stain on his honor, a girl he can't control. I've disgraced myself with Lennon and he wants rid of me any way he can. Well, he's in for a fine surprise. I stand and shake my fist at the window before grabbing a wad of tissue and wiping my face.

I hear the bathroom door open. Fiona calls out, "Penny, are you still in here?"

"Yeah," I call out before flushing the toilet.

"What's taking you so long?" she asks.

Why is she asking? Did someone tell her to come look for me? Is her unicorn love a sham so she plays the spy on her father's orders? I take a shaky breath so I don't scream. Think. I need to scheme and sham, just like them. "Have you tried using tampons with this thing on?"

"Oh." She pauses, then giggles. "Oh no. Are you okay?"

"Yeah, I guess." I step out of the stall, turn my back and lift my sparkly rainbow tail. "Any leaks?"

"No, you're good."

Even as we speak, my sham takes form. "Well, my panties aren't and your da won't let me leave."

"I can go back to the house and get you a pair."

"And more tampons, please. The heavy-duty kind."

We leave the bathroom together and she hurries ahead of me to her mother. They whisper together, eying me as I join Bridie at the dessert table. Auntie Joanne will doubtless relay this unwelcome news to Uncle Christy. It might even give them pause since their kidnappers will have to deal with an unconscious woman on the rag.

Fuckers.

I'm dizzy from not breathing, trying to contain my panic. I suck in air before whispering to Bridie, "Mum, I need you to sham right now. Act like we're talking about the food and nothing else."

"All right," she whispers as she cuts into a loaf of barm brack. Then she gasps aloud as she holds up the slice. "I got the ring."

Of course, she did. Bridie's timing has always been everything. "Great."

"I'll wear it until Matty comes back."

"Matty won't come back if you don't listen to me."

"What are you talking about?"

I tell her as she continues slicing the loaf. She keeps her face pleasant so that the only indication of her anger is her tightened grip on the knife and her breathy whisper. "I'll never forgive him for this. Fine, then. His jig is up, and we'll use his sham to our advantage."

"How?"

"After you've run off, I'll say you scarpered because you overheard his scheme. That should keep him from hunting down Lennon for a while. I'll send him on a wild goose chase."

"Won't he get mad at you?"

"So what if he does?"

"What about the mirror?"

That gives us both pause.

During our previous imprisonment in the Nest, Bridie had used a blood curse to free us, mingling her blood and the blood of our captor, Kingfisher, onto a mirror. If the mirror cracks, they both die. After Christy took over the Nest, Bridie gave the mirror to him to keep Kingfisher at bay.

Bridie exhales. "However angry he gets, he won't do anything to harm me. He's still my brother."

"Are you sure about that? Look what he has planned for me."

"I know, but I'm sure he's convinced himself he's doing it for your own good."

"His own good."

"Yes, but he'd never harm us to death. I'm certain of that." She pauses while a young mother brings her kinchin for barm brack. After they walk away, slices in hands, she whispers, "When you get to London, go to Helena. She'll help you."

"Of course." Gerry's presence brushes against me. I suck in my breath before saying, "Is there anything you want me to tell her? Her and Gareth?"

Bridie shakes her head without looking at me.

"Mum, they'll want to hear from you."

"No, they won't. I burned that bridge when I married Bill."

"No, you didn't. We should've gone to see them when we were in London."

Bridie's cheeks redden as her eyes storm with unreleased emotion. Okay, not the best topic of conversation while we're trying to sham Christy.

"They'll understand," I whisper. "Really."

She shrugs and manages a smile as a family approaches for slices of barm brack.

About ten minutes later, Fiona passes me a plastic bag containing panties and tampons. I nod my thanks and wait until she's walked away before glancing at the clock above the boxing ring. It's quarter 'til midnight and my cousin gave me the perfect excuse to linger in the loo. I glance around the room. Uncle Christy and Auntie Joanne are in each other's ears, doubtless discussing what to do about my time of the month. Bridie is standing in front of Kai, fussing with his costume while conveying our plans. I catch their eyes and see it all, worry, hope, love. I wish we shared the Silent Speech so we could wish one another Godspeed.

I stroll to the bathroom and find a queue out the door. Not good. I've no other choice but to join in. After a few minutes, a man exits the men's room across the corridor. Several of the waiting women eye each other and giggle. Then, a bolder one sticks her head in the door before calling over her shoulder, "It's empty."

I join her and two other women and go inside. The only difference between the two bathrooms is a line of urinals against the wall. I hold up the bag and say, "Do you mind?"

The other women graciously allow me to take the large end stall. I unzip the onesie, pull it off and roll it into a ball, along with the bag. Then I put on cat mask and use Bridie's lipstick to coat my lips bright red before pulling on a pair of black cat claw gloves. I wait until the last woman has left. As I reach for the stall handle, someone enters. A man, from the sound at the urinal. I wait until he's gone. Then I step out and shove the onesie into the trash, covering it with used paper towels. The door swings open and I turn to the mirror above the sink and fiddle with my mask and hair. Two more women enter and head for the stalls. As soon as they're in, I leave.

The queue of women waiting for the loo has lengthened and now includes Fiona. I pass by her, almost close enough to brush shoulders, and don't make eye contact. My heart is pounding and I'm breathless as I cross the gym and join the throng exiting outside for the midnight bonfire. It takes all my will not to glance back. Not until I'm almost out the door. I hazard a peek and see a pink unicorn still in the ladies' queue.

I chew my lip, containing an urge to giggle. Then I'm outside, breathing in the cold, damp, fresh air. In the clearing, men are removing the tarps from a huge pile of wood. Uncle Christy stands beside it, holding a lit torch, its dancing flames making his face look as red as Lucifer's. I take a few breaths to balance my *chi*, then ease away from the crowd, into the dark as I use the Stealth Skill to sneak way.

Lennon

Canny. That's the word of the day. I have to be clever and not predictable because everyone is expecting me to get on my scooter, ride to the Nest, and try to bust Penny out. I'm pretty damn sure every entrance to the Kinetic Collective is being watched by the Beggar Clan, various factions of the Two Dragon Clan, and maybe the Strowlers. It must puzzle them when the door to the loading dock rolls open and they spot me helping Junkyard Metallurgy load Doris into a moving truck. I'm dressed all in black, like the other volunteers, which hopefully adds to the confusion.

Mona grunted in response to the story of Penny's illness and my need to leave early so I can check on her. I was afraid she'd tell me to get lost since it's a lame excuse, but I guess she's too busy to care.

After we're done loading all the various pieces, I remain in the truck, seated alongside the spider's huge, creaking appendages for the ride to Civic Auditorium. It's a low-speed chase for whoever's pursuing me since traffic is moving like glue. We arrive late and the doors to Monstrosity have already opened. We unload the truck and reassemble the spider onstage behind the closed curtain as the dance hits of the '80s pound the walls. I do my best to smile and joke along with my fellow volunteers while planning my exit strategy and eyeing the shadows on the walls for any telltale shifting of energy. If anyone followed me in, they're highly skilled because I can't spot them.

We finish the assembling and stand on the sidelines while the technicians take over, checking every light and gear. I glance at my phone. No message from Penny, which hopefully means things are working out on her end. It's almost 10:30 and our show was supposed to start at 10:00. Time's running out. I need to be at the Nest by midnight. While I debate whether to leave, someone hisses, "Places."

Everything goes dark and silent as the curtain opens. Eerie music plays, softly first before growing in volume as twinkling white fairy lights appear, outlining the web. Doris's eyes glow in various shades of menacing red, as does the hourglass shape on her back. A spotlight shines on her entire body as she crawls down the web to the audience's shrieks of dismay and delight. Fishnet Fatale line up beside me, costumed as sexy witches with sharp, pointy hats and heels. They give me big sister smiles before strutting onto the stage to a dance remix of Fleetwood Mac's Rhiannon. The act involves a knight who runs onstage to do battle with the spider. He doesn't realize the witches and Doris are in a sisterhood kind of thing and, after some sexy shenanigans, the witches bind him to the web. The stage goes dark, with the spotlight on Doris descending on the flailing knight. As the audience screams and cheers, I use the Shadow Skill to disappear and slip away.

Although it's rainy and late, costumed adults crowd the streets surrounding the auditorium, partying in the alleyways like teenagers. I have to rely on the Stealth Skill rather than the Swift Step so I don't plow into any of them. The ride share lot is only a few blocks away and, once there, I use my phone to unlock the car I rented. As I reach for the handle, I sense a presence behind me. I spin around and am not at all surprised to see Big Brother.

Thick rain drops splutter down on us, but neither of us moves. We stare at each other, eyes locked in the dim light. Finally, I say, "Were we followed? I mean, you followed me, so…"

We weren't followed.

I'm not feeling super confident of that since he's using Silent Speech to communicate. *You sure?*

I didn't come alone. Our people will take out anyone who attempts to follow or attack us.

Good old Tony, always five steps ahead. *Were you inside? Did you see the spider? I helped build it.*

He waves an impatient hand. *You can't do this.*

Hell, yeah, I can. I'm the Dragon Son. You can't stop me anymore. I fold my arms and give a tight shrug. *Besides, you gave me no choice.*

What if I give you a choice? he asks without blinking.

What do you mean?

After May has our child, she and I will go to London and use the pearls to heal Matthew.

I suck in my breath. Wow. Big Brother is actually compromising. That's huge for him. *I want to say yes, but Matthew and his parents are alone and unguarded. It's only a matter of time before Uncle George attacks them and take back the Yin Pearl.*

I'll provide protection.

I thought we couldn't trust anyone at the London kongsi.

We can't. I'll ask the Beggar Clan to guard them.

That would work. We'd owe them. Again. But I'm okay with that. *I'll do it, but I'm not the only person involved. I have to ask Penny and if she agrees, we'll let you handle it.*

His arms fold and he gets that look on his face as if he'll stand there all night until he gets the answer he wants.

I gotta talk to her in person. She doesn't have her phone. I'm heading out to meet her right now.

To run away to London?

Yeah, that was the plan, but this changes things. I'm sure she'll say yes, but I gotta ask her first because, ya know, we're a team and stuff.

His frown deepens when I add 'and stuff. '*Her family will want this.*

I'm meeting her, like, right now. I gotta go. I'll call you after I talk to her. I pause because it's starting to pour. *You need a ride back to the kongsi?*

He shakes his head, steps into the shadows and disappears. Typical Tony. I hate flying in the rain, but knowing him, he sees it as an opportunity to hone his skills. I guess I should stop being mad at him now, except I'm pissed I made all these plans for nothing. To be honest, I was looking forward to having an adventure with Penny, saving the day together, that kind of thing.

And I was also looking forward to being with her... like that. And I was dreading it because it would ruin our friendship, so it's all good. Right? At this point, I don't know what I want, not until I talk to her. I climb in the car and head out.

I stick to the side streets, avoiding traffic and crowds as best I can, and park in a warehouse lot about a quarter mile from the Nest. The rain has eased, making it easier to use Swift Steps all the way to the rim of the Nest. It's surrounded by a high wire fence laced with barbs which ends where the property meets the shoreline. When I stayed there, Penny had explained that Strowlers hate being contained, so they built the fence to discourage the curious rather than keep anyone out or in. There are also security cameras, but those are easily avoided using the Stealth Skill. I ease around the barrier and head into the small forest that hides the trailer park from view, creeping through the trees until I emerge at the mouth of a small cove.

When I was hiding at the Nest, Penny and I would come out here for privacy, and to dream and scheme. Funny, how some things never change.

She's not here, but someone else is. Jade Dragon. He loves storms, winding his coiling body around the cumulous clouds and playing tag with lightning bolts. Wait. Could he be causing the bad weather?

I reach out. *Dude, can you not?*

He ignores me. Of course, he does. Dragons are weird. Don't let anyone tell you different.

Dude. For real.

Jade Dragon's presence touches mine like the swipe of a giant tail. *You have the Yang Pearl.*

Um, yeah. I glance down and realize it's glowing beneath my clothes. I cover it with my hand to tamp down the light.

Then you have all you need.

Actually, no. I found the Yin Pearl. Or rather, Penny, you know, my mate, she found it and we need to go get it.

You're going to London.

I freeze. Fucking asshole. He knew where it was all along. I take a deep breath so I don't go off on him, but I still shake my fist at the sky. *Why didn't you tell me it was there?*

I did not lose it. It was not for me to find. One of my descendants has it now and uses it to stay alive. You will take it from him?

No. That descendant, Matthew, he's Penny's stepfather. We need to use the pearls together to heal him.

Jade Dragon doesn't reply, but he remains connected to me. Waiting for something, but I don't know what. I might as well ask him about the pearls even though I know he won't be straight with me.

So, um, the Yin and Yang Pearls. How come we have to have sex to use them together?

You don't.

I freeze again. Is he kidding? No, dragons don't kid. *What?*

Two must be connected as one through the Silent Speech to use the pearls together.

But not through sex? He doesn't answer because he already did. *When you say two, do you mean the Dragon Son and his wife?*

I mean any two humans. My descendants interpreted my instructions as they saw fit.

Why didn't you tell them they had it wrong?

They did not ask. The Dragon Son wanted to keep the power for himself. This interested me, though the results were as expected and became less interesting, until the Yin Pearl was lost.

This dragon… we're not even pawns to him because he doesn't move us around. *We're like specimens under your microscope*

No. You are my descendants. I watch your progress and evolution. You seek knowledge. You ask. Your wisdom increases. If you do not, you become weak and diminished.

I have to ask. *Did my dad become weak?*

He feared me and that made him weak. We spoke little because that fear made it impossible for us to communicate.

Did you know that he found the Wisdom Pearl?

Yes.

Does my uncle have it now?

Yes.

And that confirms it. Damn. All this knowledge he just spilled would have saved me a truckload of grief. What do I do now? Wait for May to have her baby so she and Tony can go to London? Can Matthew last that long?

Howls and cheers sound in the distance. I turn and see an orange glow over the top of the trees. That must be some epic bonfire. Then, from the gloom of the forest, a black cat appears, moving with the subtle grace of a dancer. Penny pulls off her mask and her pale face glows like the moon amidst the darkness. She smiles and my heart soars.

"Hey," she breathes out as she comes up next to me. "We

gotta go. We don't have much time before they realize I'm gone."

I don't want to tell her Tony's offer, but I can't be an asshole like that. "We have to talk first."

"There's no time to talk. They could be here any minute."

"I know, but this is important." Where to start? First things first. "Tony caught up with me while I was sneaking away. He said he and May would use the pearls to heal Matthew after the baby is born."

Penny's eyes widen as her mouth drops open. "No. This can't wait. You don't understand. I found out that Uncle Christy is planning to have me kidnapped and kept prisoner in another Nest."

Now my mouth drops open. "What? No. He can't do that."

"He can and he will if I stay here."

"Then, let's go."

Her eyes narrow as my hand drops from my chest. "What's that light around your neck? Is it your phone?"

Should I tell her? Might as well since it's the other thing we need to talk about. "The Yang Pearl. It's glowing because Jade Dragon is here."

"Where?"

I gesture at the horizon. "Out there somewhere, but close."

"Why can't I see him? Is he invisible?"

"No, he's using the Stealth Skill. Our clan learned it from him."

She eyes the Yang Pearl again before saying, "What does he want?"

"I don't know. But, he told me something important…"

She gasps abruptly, her face going blank as if from shock.

"Penny? What is it?"

"The dragon," she whispers. "He's talking to me. He's real."

Hey, I mind-shout at Jade Dragon. *Whatever you're doing to Penny, cut it out.*

"No, it's okay. I recognize him. He's the one who helped me escape from your uncle. He wants to know what we're doing."

"I already told him."

"He wants to hear it from me." She closes her eyes.

I wrap my arms around her. She's tense, but also relaxed, as if in a semi-trance. *Cut it out.*

Jade Dragon ignores me, of course, but so does Penny. In the distance, I hear voices shouting her name. I take a deep breath and concentrate my *chi* so I can connect with both of them. *They're coming. We have to go.*

Penny opens her eyes and smiles. *It's all right. He's going to help us.*

Is that even a good idea? *Help us how?*

The ground disappears from beneath my feet as I'm sucked into some kind of vortex that rushes me upward. I try grasping for Penny, but I can't move. Pressure surrounds me, making me nauseous, as if I'm trapped in speeding elevator, but much worse. I want to scream or speak, but I can't. Even the Silent Speech is denied me. Finally, I'm settled onto something, except settled isn't the right word. The thing moves. It coils. It's cold and scaly and undulates as it moves through the sky. I'm on Jade Dragon, straddling his back. Penny is in front of me and I wrap my arms around her. She grips my knees, her fingers digging in so tight I can feel her nails. Some kind of energy bubble is keeping us in place, restricting our movement, and protecting us from the frozen air and high altitude. I close my eyes and take deep, calming breaths to slow my pounding heart. Then I open and finally see Jade Dragon.

He looks like a dragon. I mean, yeah, I know, but for some reason, I thought he'd look different. Imagine a blue, scaly sea serpent the size of an airplane, but with four legs, a silky mane, horns and gills, and a head that looks like a cross between a camel and a lion. He doesn't have wings since he flies through the power of his ancient *chi* ability, much of which is stored in the immense pearl glowing at his throat.

Penny twists around to look at me. Her face is white as a sheet and her eyes shine like emeralds, yet she looks serene, like a fairy princess atop her steed. Her mind gently touches mine. *Don't be afraid.*

I'm not. Yeah, right. *What's he doing?*

Taking us to London.

Penny

I've never seen the stars shine so bright before. Not even the night Gerry parked our caravan beside a country road on our way to a gig in Aberdeen. After a late supper, we all went to bed, but I was still restless from the long drive. After an hour of tossing and turning, I got up and Kai followed. I opened the door, and we stepped out to a crisp autumn night that smelled of fallen leaves, hay, and Highland cow shit. We looked up, dazzled by the myriad of diamond-like stars set against the inky sky. Such beauty. If only it could last forever, but moments later, headlights appeared on the horizon. A line of cars barreled up the road and screeched to a halt, surrounding our caravan. Men jumped out, yelling about filthy pikeys and demanding we leave. Gerry and Matthew stayed back, allowing Bridie to weave her spell, pouring Charm into their ears, persuading them to leave us be. Would things have been different for us, for Strowlers, if we'd had dragon power as well?

I ask Jade Dragon *Do you know Master Stoorworm?*

Yes, he replies in a voice that's a cross between a hiss and a rumble. Not animal-like, but not human, either.

Is he still alive?

Stoorworm abides in the deep and awaits the day.

What does that mean? Again, I wait, but there's no response. I don't want to prod him because I don't know what it will take for him to shake us off his back. I don't think he will since he's gone this far to help us, but why take any chances? What do I know about dragons or any of this, except that I'm terrified and half-convinced it's all a dream? I hazard another question. *Lennon and I need to use the Yin and Yang pearls to heal my father, but we don't know how. Can you tell us?*

Knowledge flashes through my mind like lightning, step-by-step instructions on how to use the Yin Pearl imprinted in my memory so I'll never forget, finishing with, *To achieve the Dragon Touch, you and your mate must be sealed by the Silent Speech. The bond of intercourse is unnecessary.*

Did I hear that right? *What?*

The dragon doesn't reply. I can't tell if I'm relieved or disappointed. It's like the world is conspiring to tear us apart while throwing us together at every chance. Maybe I need to see it as one last thing to worry about. I want to tell Lennon, but the dragon isn't finished with me yet.

Where do you feel safe?

That's a hard question to answer, riding on the back of a dragon above... I glance over the side. Is that the Atlantic Ocean? Where do I feel safe? Not here. Not anywhere. The apartment is San Francisco never felt like home. Strowler Nests feel like traps, waiting to swallow me into an arranged marriage. The Wayward Way encampments never felt safe since they attracted volatile people with nowhere else to go on the Crossroads. I've never truly felt safe, not with my parents nor even with Lennon because there's nothing safe about him. He's a walking bundle of danger. Maybe that's why I'm so attracted to him. Danger feels more real to me than safety.

The sky grows lighter and grayer as we head east. All at

once, the sun pierces out from the curve of the earth. At the same moment, a translucent layer darkens the protective shield surrounding me and Lennon. It reminds of a lizard's eyelid and makes me wonder if Jade Dragon has such a lid protecting his eyes. I reach out and touch the shield. It's cool with a serrated smoothness.

It's like touching a snake, I tell Lennon.

He reaches out and lays his palm on the shield. *Jade Dragon is using the energy from his pearl to protect us. That, plus carrying us this far is putting a huge strain on him. He can't keep it up for much longer.*

How long do we have?

I don't know. Lennon pauses. *Okay, I asked, and he said, long enough.*

I hope so. Before my fear can work itself into a lather, I spot land below and realize its jagged coast of Ireland. How long have we been flying? It feels like minutes have passed, but also like days have gone by, almost as if we'd spent the night dancing with the fairies, only to discover in the morning that a hundred years have passed.

Jade Dragon prods me again. I sift through memories, trying to find places where I'd felt safe, even for a few precious moments. Someplace sweet, green, and fun, with laughter and food, but otherwise unremarkable.

I capture the moment and Jade Dragon swoops downward in a graceful arc. Lennon and I grab hold of each other even though we're still held in place. We move through a cloud bank before bursting out above the gray drizzle of a London morning. I spot the Thames, Big Ben, Westminster Abbey, and all the various landmarks. We're really here and we're really going to save Matthew. I twist around to look at Lennon and I notice the Yang Pearl is glowing brighter. I point and he looks down, frowning.

What the...

The glow intensifies, brighter and brighter, so I have to close my eyes against the burning radiance. Energy thrums from its core and surges through our bodies. I want to scream, but terror is overcome by exhilaration and the sense I can do anything, even step off Jade Dragon's back and fly. Then the energy subsides until it becomes just a burning pin prick in the center of my chest.

I hear geese honking, but they're not flying alongside us. They're gliding across a round blue pond. We're no longer on the dragon's back. We're sitting on a wooden bench. A man in running gear gives us an odd look as he jogs past as if we'd appeared out of thin air.

Did we?

Lennon sucks in air and gives his head a vigorous shake. "Where are we?"

"Hyde Park." I glance around and give my head a shake too. "Wow."

"What?"

"Jade Dragon asked me where I feel safe. This is the exact spot where my family used to come and have picnics and feed the birds. We even called this our bench. See." I scoot over to show him where Gerry had carved Wild Sky with his pocket knife.

"So that's why he dropped us off here?"

"I guess. He didn't tell me."

"No. He wouldn't. He's kind of a dick."

"Where is he now?"

Lennon squints for a silent moment before saying, "He's on top of a church or something. He's shrunk to the size of a bird and he's resting."

I squint, too, and rub at the still-burning pinprick in my chest as I sense Jade Dragon's presence. I try communicating, but he ignores me. "Actually, he's at the Tower, which is more like a castle, and he's hanging out with the ravens."

"That'll keep him busy for a while." He rubs his chest as well. "Do you feel different?"

"Yeah, like, I should be exhausted, but I have all this energy, but it's more than that…" I trail off and shake my head because I don't know.

Lennon pulls his buzzing phone out of his pocket. "Crap. Tony and Bridie have been blowing up my phone for the last two hours."

So that's how long it takes a dragon to fly from San Francisco to London. Good to know. "Let me see." He hands me the phone and I scroll through my mother's increasingly hysterical messages before I tap out a reply.

> It's me. Penny. Sorry. We've been on the move and couldn't stop. We're safe now and on our way to London. Are you all right?

> Thank God!!! You could have taken a moment to answer me, but I understand. You're on a plane?

I hate to lie, but I have little choice.

> Yes. We just boarded. Are you all right?

> We're fine. Christy's gone spare. He kicked us out of the Nest.

> What happened?

> I told him you whiddled his scheme and legged it with my blessing. We had a row, and he declared us shunned. It's all right. We're back at our apartment.

Is that a good thing, though? Outside the safety of the Nest, she and Kai can become a target once George realizes we have the Yin Pearl. I show Lennon her messages. "We need to protect them."

He nods. "I'll tell Tony."

> Stay put. Don't go out unless you have to.
> Lennon will have Tony protect you.

> Good. I was feeling nervous here on our own.
> When do you get to London?

> I need to give Lennon the phone so he can
> text Tony before we take off. I love you!

I hand him the phone. Then I lean back and close my eyes while he communicates with Tony. I need to chill out, but I'm so keyed up, I want to run circles around Round Pond while shouting at the geese and swans. I almost would except I'm also starving, like I could eat one of those geese.

"Okay," says Lennon. "I told Tony everything he needs to know."

"Did you tell him we don't have to… you know… do it?"

He looks down. "Jade Dragon told you?"

"Yeah."

"I was going to tell you."

"I know." He's being silly and awkward, but I can't blame him since I feel the same way.

He shrugs. "I told Tony. He's still not happy, but Tony doesn't do happy." He gnaws his lip. "This is gonna sound weird, but I'm super hungry. Like, starved."

"Me, too. There's a cafe nearby, let's go there."

I lead the way along the leaf-strewn pathways of Hyde Park, passing Kensington Palace and the statue of Queen Victoria. Lennon gawks but doesn't linger because, like me, he's driven by ravenous hunger demanding to be fed. Outside the park, we cross Bayswater Road and stop at an ATM so we can take out cash before heading into the nearest cafe.

Lennon's eyes goggle and I don't blame him or anyone who steps in here for the first time. Floor to ceiling, every available surface is covered with photos of Princess Diana, including our table.

As we sit at our table, Lennon says, "I'll have whatever you're having."

I turn to the waiter. "Two Full English, coffee, and two croissants for right now."

His bushy gray eyebrows lift. "Plain, chocolate, or almond?"

I want to say all three, but settle for, "Chocolate. Thanks." I turn to Lennon. "Full English has stewed tomatoes and baked beans. Hope that's okay."

"Yeah. I've had it in Hong Kong."

I almost forgot his family is from there. That's something we have in common, being descended from people subjugated by the British. The waiter returns with our coffees and croissants, and we devour every flakey morsel. After that, and a refill of coffee, I can think a little clearer.

So can Lennon. He glances around and whispers, "We couldn't eat someplace less creepy?"

"Princess Diana lived at Kensington Palace, so…" I spread my hands.

"So… still creepy."

I won't argue with that. We need to talk, but I want no one overhearing, so I use the Silent Speech. *Do you still feel that energy? I mean, kind of like a pinprick in your chest?*

Yeah. I think Jade Dragon gave us some of his chi.

Why would he do that?

I'm not sure. I've been thinking about it. Dragons don't help their young, but that doesn't mean he won't help you.

So, he's helping me so I can help you?

Maybe? He sighs. *I've been talking to the guy for years, and I still don't get him. Dragons are different. Obviously. What I mean is,* he's not human, at all, so whatever he does might make sense to him, but not to us.

Breakfast arrives and the smell of fried eggs, crisp-skin sausage, and baked beans overwhelms my ability to speak. We dig in and after some of that hunger is satisfied, I tell him about my conversation with Jade Dragon.

He told me everything except what to do afterward. That worries me because I have a feeling Air Dragon is a one-way flight.

Lennon shakes his head. *I told you. He likes to watch us struggle and figure things out.*

Even it means we could die?

Especially if it means that.

I almost take another sip of coffee but set the cup down. Even after all that food, I'm still feeling super-charged and more caffeine won't help. *Okay, here's the thing. We didn't enter the UK legally and our passports will show that, which means we won't be able to buy tickets to fly home unless we get some help.*

What kind of help?

The Beggar kind.

You mean the London Beggar Clan? Won't they tell Jeremiah we're here?

No, they won't. The Beggar Chief and her brother were… are friends of my family.

Friends enough to go against the interest of their clan?

I look down. It's still hard to talk about, even now. Secrets held close, never to be revealed because… I suck in my breath. *Helena and Gareth would never betray me. They'll want to help Matthew. It won't hurt having someone watching our backs while we heal him. Otherwise, we're going into this alone with no one to help if we're attacked.*

True, but I don't want then knowing about the pearls.

I'll tell them what we told Christy, that Matthew's still alive and you have the power to heal him. I shrug. *It's not a lie. If they ask me how, I'll say I can't tell them because it's a clan secret. Also not a lie.*

He stares at his empty plate and takes a deep breath before looking up and nodding. *If it's the quickest, best way to help Matthew, then that's what we'll do.*

Thank you. I reach out and take his hand. A surge of power passes between us. I'm surprised we don't light up.

He grins, kind of crazy because his eyes are dazzled. I wonder if I look the same. I must, since the waiter is giving us a leery look. Maybe he thinks we're high and we sort of are, on Dragon Juice. I wonder how long this will last? We need to get to Matthew as soon as possible.

"So, you know where to go?" Lennon asks after we leave the cafe.

I nod and raise my hand to hail an approaching taxi. As we climb in, I say to the driver, "Grey Coat Hospital."

Lennon

As we drive through the streets of London, I feel like I'm returning to the scene of the crime. Why do I feel this weird guilt? I'm not responsible for what happened to Auntie Cat's mom or Penny's dads, or am I? Everything seems tied to keeping Dad's dirty secrets so I can be the Dragon Son. I distract myself by glancing around. London reminds me of Hong Kong with its mix of old and new buildings. We pass Buckingham Palace and I'm disappointed because it's not as grand as I thought it would be. It looks like a hotel. I don't want to offend our driver, so I use Silent Speech.

Is it nicer on the inside?

Penny grins. *I guess. I've never been in there or any of the palaces. We don't give a toss about the royals.*

Not surprising since on the Crossroads, clan rule has more authority than any governing body. *Are there a lot of clans in London?*

Oh yeah. The biggest one is the Beggar Clan.

What about the Templars?

She shudders. *Nasty, violent buggers.*

Are they any danger to us?

Them? No. During their glory days, they were the head clan of the Crossroads in most of western Europe. Then their star fell, hard. That was… She thinks before waving a hand. *800 years ago or something. Nowadays, they keep to themselves, except for when they're having a go at one of the Muslim clans, which is basically all the time. Some things never change.*

She's talking about the Crusades. Most Crossroads clans steer clear of the politics of the day, but some get caught up in the turmoil and even throw in their support, like the Dragon Son and his wife during the Taiping Rebellion.

Anyway, she continues, *after the Templars fell, the Beggar Clan took over and were head clan of the Crossroads until everything got, I don't know, globalized, and the Two Dragon Clan came along. Thing is, it doesn't matter who the actual head of the Crossroads is. The Beggar Clan reigns supreme in London.*

Yeah, I know. Same in Beijing, Rome, Tripoli, or any ancient city. The Two Dragon Clan is an upstart punk compared to them. If we didn't have a dragon for an ancestor who jacked up our *chi* abilities, we'd be just another small, obscure Chinese clan. The Beggar Clan is far more numerous and helps people in need. That's why I planned to lose to John Walks Long. He'd have been the best Head of the Crossroads ever. Jeremiah… I don't know that he's all that bad, but he's not his father and never will be, just like I'll never be my father.

Penny breaks back into my morose thoughts. *In England, the head of the Beggar Clan in any city is called Poor Tom.*

Isn't that confusing?

No. He's referred to as London Tom or York Tom, depending on the city. There are variations, like in Birmingham where he's called Brummie Tom. And if the head of the clan is a woman, she's called Mad Maud.

Have there been a lot of women chiefs?

Yeah. Back in the day, Poor Tom's wife was called Mad Maud and if he died an untimely death, she took over the role of chief. Nowa-

days, chiefs are chosen by election, same as in SF. She pauses long enough for me to think she's finished before continuing. *So, the current Mad Maud, she's been chief for a few years, but I've known her all my life. Her real name is Helena. Her brother, Gareth, he and Gerry... They were close.*

How close?

She sucks in her breath. *They were in love. Planning to get married.*

I blink hard. Oh. Shit. *Why didn't you tell me this before?*

She looks out the window. *Because it's hard. Painful. There was this whole other life I was supposed to live and didn't. I don't like talking about it. Even thinking about it hurts.*

I understand. I really do. *Same with after my parents died.*

I know. She clasps my hand. A low-key electrical surge passes between us. The long we hold on, the stronger it grows, so we let go. It's not a bad feeling, but it's intense. The feelings I have for Penny are intense enough. I don't need the boost.

The cab drops us off in front of an old brick building on a street full of old brick buildings with slanted roofs and square-paned windows. I squint at the sign above the door.

Grey Coat Hospital
Church of England
Comprehensive School for Girls

"Is this a hospital or a school?"

"It's a school," says Penny. "Back in the day, hospital meant any institution that served the poor."

Now I get it. Or do I? "The Beggar Clan's headquarters is in a girls' school?"

"Nope. Follow me."

We head down the street, along the length of the school/hospital, until we reach the corner and another red brick building. This one is smaller and more modern looking, built in the early 20th century if judging by the arched entrance with its Art Deco glass inlay. Above that is a white marble plaque inlaid in black with the words *Grey Coat Station*. Below the arch is a plain metal sign reading, *The Hearth*. On either side of the opening are two display cases. One says:

Underground Electric Trains to all Parts of London.

The other:

The Hearth
Homeless Advocacy
Your Home on the Street

A line of men, women, and children stretches from the kiosk inside the entrance to around the next block.

Is this a train station or a soup kitchen? I ask.

It's the Beggar Abode. She taps her foot and I see the Beggar Clan road marker, an open rectangle with three circles, scraped into the sidewalk when the cement had still been wet.

London is full of abandoned train lines and stations. This one closed in the fifties. The clan bought it in the sixties and converted the building into a homeless shelter. It's the perfect sham because the Beggars can come and go with no one noticing.

Is that why you didn't have the cab stop here?

She nods. I get it. Dropping off two kids in front of a homeless shelter would seem odd, noticeable, something the driver might talk about in the wrong place to the wrong person.

I follow Penny as she approaches a man standing beside the kiosk. He's wearing jeans and a green T-shirt printed with the words HEARTH STAFF. The friendly smile he has for the homeless fades as we approach.

He shakes his head. "Sorry, kids, we're not open for school assignments. Try Saint Paul's."

"We're not students," says Penny. "Walk in peace."

His eyes narrow as he looks from her to me, so I say, "Walk in peace."

Suspicion remains on his face. "Walk in peace. What do you want?"

"Penny Sparrow to see Mad Maud."

"Sparrow. You're a Strowler."

She nods.

He turns to me. "And you?"

"I'm not."

He doesn't blink as he adjusts his mouthpiece and turns away to speak into it. Then he gestures for us to look up at a wall-mounted camera. Penny gives a little wave and I flash a peace sign because why not? The guard listens for a few moments before gesturing us to follow him.

The inside of the station looks like a cafeteria. Smiling, green-shirted Beggars direct their guests to the long metal tables or to the counter where more green shirts serve food from huge, steaming trays. Small queues are also forming outside doors marked, "First Aid" and "Employment and Housing." Why doesn't the Two Dragon Clan do something like this? We used to serve the community, from the old stories I've heard, until power and money became more important. That's gonna change now I'm the new sheriff in town. We could learn a lot from the Beggar Clan. They might be the oldest clan on the Crossroads, but in a lot of ways, they're the most modern, the one that moves with the times.

At the end of the room, we're handed off to two staff with sterner faces. They flank us as another green shirt opens a sliding metal gate. We head down a tube-shaped stairwell decorated with white, gold, and green ceramic tiles and enter a long, wide corridor inlaid with the words *Grey Coat Station* and arrows pointing toward the other end. As we walk, we pass Beggars going through their morning exercises. Some are doing fitness routines while others spar atop foam mats. From the tattoos, grim faces, and haunted eyes, most seem to be former military, just like in SF. The walls vibrate from the rush of trains whizzing by on adjacent lines. Do they live here? How do they not go crazy from the racket? Maybe after a while it becomes white noise.

At the end of the corridor, we reach a platform where old-fashioned, red subways cars with curtained windows sit on the track, stretching into the tunnel in either direction. On the wall behind the trains, I can see fading, peeling posters advertising cigarettes, Ovaltine, and Spam.

I feel like I stepped back in time, I tell Penny.

You sort of have, she replies. *When the station was abandoned, they left the trains on the tracks and never came back to get them. The Beggars turned them into living quarters.*

No surprise, because no one is more resourceful with junk than the Beggar Clan.

Our escort leads us down the platform to another, smaller corridor marked with a fancy, art deco-style sign saying No Exit. As advertised, there is no exit at the end, but an elevator the size of a small coat closet. We cram in and head down in a slow, creaking rattling motion. It seems like a long way down and when we get there, we step even further back in time. Thick grey bricks and industrial steel for the tube-shaped wall making the place feel more like a dungeon. The small train on the tracks looks almost like a carnival ride. It's painted green and red, and has a clear, plexiglass cover.

Where are we and what is that? I ask.

That's a mail train. They used to haul mail to stations around London on the mail rail line. During World War 2, this station was turned into a secret back-up bunker for Winston Churchill and the Cabinet in case the one near Downing Street took a direct hit in the Blitz. It was boarded up and forgotten after the war until the Beggars found it.

I glance at the cable running from the engine to what looks like an electric meter. *Does it still run?*

Maybe? That's not something they've told me.

I can feel the weight of history as we follow the guard into a long, narrow mail sorting room with hundreds of empty slots lining the walls, through a door and into a corridor built with bricks, wood beams, and sturdy, square air ducts. Filing cabinets line walls hung with clocks, maps, and a framed black-and-white photo of a guy in a uniform who I'm guessing was the king. The guard holds up his hand as we come to the first door which is open. He knocks anyway and motions for us to step inside.

Maps of Europe, Africa, and Asia, with the Axis powers' subjugated territories marked, cover the walls from floor to ceiling. Those and the furnishings must all be from the war, including the desk, banker lamps, and dial phone with its bright green receiver. I want to ask if this was Churchill's office, but I don't think they'll tell me.

'They' are a man and a woman, who come to their feet as we enter. The woman must be Mad Maud. She's younger and shorter than I expected with a pointy, pixie face beneath a pile of ratted, bushy reddish-gold hair held in place by an assortment of brightly colored hair clips. Like all Beggar Chiefs, she wears her poverty proudly with a skirt made from ripped and patched denim jackets, a blue sweater with enough gaping holes to show the white T-shirt beneath, and dirty, fingerless gloves that looked decades old. Her knee-high, side-buckled brown leather boots seem almost as old, though the thick rubber soles appear new. Her staff, a chipped wooden cane with a worn brass handle, leans against her desk.

The man beside her has redder hair and bluer eyes, and is about six inches taller, but his pointy features identify him as Mad Maud's brother. He's shaved and trimmed, and dressed in form-fitting, casual clothes, meaning he's one who infiltrates the mundane world.

Mad Maud opens her arms and Penny rushes in for a hug. Her fond smile fades as she fixes suspicious eyes on me.

Penny moves on to the man, who closes his eyes and hold on tight, his face squeezed with emotion. He seems reluctant to let go as she steps away. "What are you doing here?" His voice is low and concerned. He gestures at me with his chin. "With him?"

Penny steps between us and clears her throat. "Um… this is Lennon Lau… He's… um…"

"The Dragon Son," the Beggar Chief finishes for her. She nods at me. "Walk in peace."

"Walk in peace." I nod to her and her brother, who nods back with a frown.

"Jeremiah and John Walks Long both told me about you," says Mad Maud. "They said you were unusual."

I shrug. They walk around carrying staffs and wearing rags, and I'm the weirdo.

"They also told me you and Penny had become friends and persisted in that friendship, despite all warnings." She turns to Penny. "Why are you here with him?" She holds up a hand. "No, wait. I want to hear from you alone. Gareth, take our guest and wait outside."

Penny and I exchange looks before I follow Gareth out. I can feel her reluctance to sham people she loves and trusts. Now, I have to trust her, that she won't tell them. Gareth shuts the door behind us as we enter the corridor. We lean against opposite walls and he looks at me with narrowed eyes, like a cat about to pounce.

"You're from San Francisco, yeah?" he asks.

"Yeah."

"You like it?"

"Sure."

"Did you know Penny's father was gay?"

Okay, that's what this is about. Being from SF doesn't mean I'm not some asshole bigot. "Yeah. I don't care. I mean, being gay, bi, trans, it's great. Um…" Should I say? Might as well. "Penny told me you and Gerry were, like, close."

His mouth quirks as his head tilts to the side. If he had a tail, it would be swishing. "Yeah, we were close. We'd been on and off for years while I was in the military. When I got my discharge, we decided to make a go of it, and live together, and maybe even get married and then…" Air hisses through his teeth. He tilts back his head and stares at the jigsaw ceiling of ducts and beams. "Gerry was a mad bastard. He loved taking risks. Probably the smartest man I ever met, and he could barely read, but he could sing and play any instrument, and he could pick a lock with a paperclip. He'd do anything for those he loved, and he loved Matthew. I don't know what they were up to that night. He didn't say a word. We were supposed to meet at Wilde's, a bar in Soho. He'd said he had great news, but he never showed up."

"I'm sorry," I whisper.

"Are you?" His eyes lock with mine. "We always suspected it had something to do with the Two Dragon Clan. Know anything about that?"

"No. I mean, I was a kid. No one told me about stuff like that."

"What about now?"

The door opens and Mad Maud pokes her head out. Her eyes are full of tears.

Gareth peals himself off the wall. "Helena, what's wrong?"

She shakes her head and takes a breath before gesturing him inside. The door closes behind them. It looks like the Beggar Chief knows Matthew is alive. From her reaction, they must've all been good friends. I think of Bridie as Penny's mom, but she had this whole other life when she was young, a life not too different from me and Penny. You'd think they'd understand us instead of judging and blocking us.

After a few minutes, the door opens again and a red-eyed Gareth motions me in. He and his sister stand with Penny between them as if they want to protect her from me.

Mad Maud clears her throat. "You can heal Matthew?"

I nod.

"How?"

"I can't tell you. I can only say it's part of my power as the Dragon Son." She doesn't look convinced, so I continue. "Penny probably told you this wasn't my idea or hers. Matthew's parents requested my help. I can do it, but it won't be easy, and I'll need backup because my uncle is trying to kill me."

"I still don't understand why Matthew's parents faked his death. Penny said it had something to do with what he and Gerry were trying to steal, but she won't tell me what."

"I can't tell you, either."

"You're asking a lot."

"I know." I chew my lip. If she's going to risk lives, she needs to know more. "Matthew still has the thing he and Gerry stole that night. That's why his parents have kept him hidden."

"Ah." Maud's eyes light up with this knowledge. "That's why you're helping Penny."

Gareth glares at me. "You said you didn't know anything about it."

"I didn't. Not until Matthew's parents told Penny, and she told me. I don't know who killed them."

"He's telling the truth," says Penny. "Please. Will you help us?"

"Of course," replied Maud, her eyes softening. "I'll do anything to help your family." She turns to me. Something about her expression tells me she's going to say the four words I've come to hate. "I knew your father."

I grind my teeth.

"He came to London for my first Beggars' Banquet as chief. He was a charming, powerful man." She gives me a once over. "You're nothing like him."

Ouch, I guess? Is she poking needles in me to see where I bleed?

"He was famous for being righteous, but it turns out he was fooling everyone. Does the apple fall far from the tree?"

How do I respond to that? "Um, after he died, I fell and rolled down a hill, and I've just kept rolling."

She and Gareth squint like I've confused them. Good.

Penny winks. *Don't say anything else. Let her chew on that.*

Okay. I have nothing else to say, anyway.

Mad Maud reaches for a tablet on her desk and swipes. "I'll need time to mobilize the troops. We should be ready by 13:00 hours."

Penny exhales. "Thank you."

I don't give thanks because it's more than that for me. "I'm in your debt, Beggar Chief."

The chief shakes her head. "It's in the best interest of our clan you remain the Dragon Son. Consider this my effort on your behalf."

Which is to say she'll let me know when the debt is due.

Penny

Since we entered the Abode, I've felt Gerry's presence again, so close. Did Jade Dragon knowingly give his spirit a ride? Or is he somehow clinging to me, waiting for this moment? A song of joy and sting of sorrow resounded through me when I first saw Gareth. Then Gerry left me and hovered near his love while I spoke to Maud. Now, I feel as though he's somewhere in-between, waiting.

Gareth takes us back to the lift. Inside, I wrap my arms around him. As he hugs me back, I feel it, an actual physical sensation, as if Gerry were hugging us both. Gareth's soft gasp tells me he feels it, too. Then the sensation fades away and so does Gerry's spirit. Is this what he's been waiting for? Tears fill my eyes and sobs shake my body. I don't want to lose him again.

A faint whisper floats across my consciousness, *It's still Samhain, love.*

I almost forgot. We'll have him with us until midnight. Long enough to see his best friend healed. I exhale and smile. Tears dampen my hair as Gareth kisses the top of my head.

"I missed you, Penny Lane," he says in a hoarse whisper.

"I missed you, too, Pa."

He makes a noise, something between a chuckle and a sob. Gerry was Da and Matthew was Ba, so Gareth was dubbed Pa. It's a lovely, painful memory, one I've kept suppressed since that horrible night when everything changed.

The lift rattles and shudders to a halt. I glance over at Lennon with his folded arms and bowed head. I know he's blaming himself. I want to reach out and tell him to stop, but it can wait for a private moment.

We follow Gareth through a series of corridors to the platform of another station that had been built but never used or even named. Decommissioned trains on either side of the tracks, abandoned over fifty years ago, sit as a testament to bureaucratic waste and Beggar Clan ingenuity. My throat tightens as we pass carriages with open doors and curtains, and I can make out Beggars and their families going about their morning routine. I stop before we reach the last train.

Gareth looks at me with concerned eyes. "Are you all right?"

I shrug. "Yeah. It's just… memories."

"Sorry. It's the only carriage available. I can try finding someplace else."

I shake my head. "It's okay."

He opens the door and motions Lennon inside. Then he looks me in the eyes with that crystal blue gaze. "Whoever did this to us will pay."

I nod and watch as he walks away. I don't have to close my eyes to picture Gerry beside him, their hands almost touching. The time had never been right for them. They first met right before I was born and neither of them was free. When Beggars come of age in the UK, they join the military. It's a thing with them. You have to be a soldier before you can be a Beggar. Gareth decided to be extra and went to university first to become a doctor. The military paid for his education and he had to pay them back with service. Either we'd been traveling, or Gareth had been posted somewhere far away like Iraq or Afghanistan. When he finally left the military, the first thing he and Gerry did was go on holiday to Spain. I was afraid Gerry would leave us for good, but I was glad, too. I wanted them to be happy. But Gerry couldn't bear leaving us, so they decided to buy another caravan, where he and Gareth would live. Gareth would fulfill his Beggar Clan duties while in London and go with us when we traveled. It was the best of all possible worlds, except it never happened.

Gareth embodies a golden moment when everything was perfect for my family until it shattered completely. If I can face him again, I can re-enter this carriage.

Inside, Lennon is poking around the car with obvious fascination. The frame is in its original condition with green metal walls, wood-paneled windows, and hardwood floors. Vintage tube maps and adverts serve as decoration though only because this is a guest house. The Beggars add personal touches to their own carriages. A row of the original seats with their dark maroon checkerboard pattern remain intact, but the rest of the benches were torn out and replaced with a kitchenette, a bathroom, curtained bunkbeds, and a private bedroom.

Lennon goes to the sink and turns on the spigot. He blinks at the water pouring out. "There's plumbing. Man, the Beggars have their shit together." He turns and looks at me with a pinched brow. "You okay?"

I shake my head. "This is where we hid after Gerry and Matthew died."

He gapes before saying, "Oh wow."

I sit, drawing my knees to my chest. Tears don't come, maybe because I'm all cried out.

"You want to wait outside instead?" he asks, perching beside me.

I shake my head. "It's not so much that we'd stayed here. It's that I didn't want to leave. Bridie said no, that we had to return to our home Nest in Ireland. I was so angry, until I realized she was protecting Gareth. After Gerry died, there was an attempt on Gareth's life. We didn't know who it was, but we suspected Gerry's oldest brother, Oren, wanting to blame someone for him being gay. So, Bridie made herself an open target by returning to the Nest."

"But wasn't she already scandalous for living with two men?"

"Yeah, but that's not an unusual situation on the Wayward Way, where there are more men than women. Don't get me wrong, Glory Road types don't like it, but it won't get you killed. The gay stuff will, even now, so Bridie allowed the Kestrels to vent their spleen on her, until it got to be too much and then she took up with Bill, and we moved to America."

"I'm sorry," Lennon whispers. "It's my clan's fault this happened."

I shrug because I don't blame the Two Dragon Clan. "I blame Matthew's parents. They should've sucked it up instead of asking Gerry and Matthew to do something so dangerous." I feel a ghost of a nudge and gasp. "Gerry and Gareth wanted their own caravan. Those aren't cheap. The Wongs must've offered Gerry enough money to buy one."

"Gareth told me he was supposed to meet Gerry at a bar that night and that Gerry said he had good news."

I fold my arms across my tightened chest. My gritted teeth keep me from responding. The Wongs have been our puppet masters, manipulating our every move. I can't wait to cut those strings with the sharpest knife.

Lennon pulls out his phone and stares at the screen. "Still blowing up. Tony and Bridie want to know when our plane lands."

"What should we say?"

"I'm not saying anything to Tony. He'll freak if he finds out I'm with the Beggar Clan."

"Anything I say will freak Bridie out, so, yeah, let's wait until after we heal Matthew. Then they can freak out all they want."

"Speaking of which, what did Jade Dragon tell you about using the pearls?"

I open my mouth, but words won't come. That low key energy humming through me intensifies. Without thought, I close my eyes and lift my hand, palm out, to Lennon. His cold, calloused fingertips touch mine. Then our palms press as our minds connect. It's like the Silent Speech, but it's not because the knowledge flows as if transmitted from the dragon using me as a receptor. I lose all sense of my body, but it's not frightening. It just is. Then I realize I'm not breathing. I inhale and my eyelids flutter as my senses return. Lennon and I are standing, facing each other, both hands touching palm-to-palm.

Lennon's eyes blink open. "Okay, that was intense."

Intense isn't a strong enough word. It still feels like we're inhabiting the same skin. Our fingers curl as our hands clasp and squeeze. It isn't enough to contain what's between us. We embrace, our bodies pressing together as our kisses deepen with passion. It's like we can't be close enough. Something more than sexual desire is driving us, some kind of dragon energy within. On the edge of my consciousness, I feel Gerry's ghost. He's not happy. Of course, he's not. I put my hands on Lennon's shoulder and push him away.

We stare at each other, red-faced and panting. I look down as he stumbles through apologies and wave my hand. "It wasn't just you. It's like I couldn't control myself."

"Yeah," he breathes out. He stares at his shoes.

"Really. It's okay." Who knows what would have happened if my ghost of a father wasn't here? Another few moments and we might have wound up in bed. The tingling parts of my body wish we had.

There's a knock on the door and we jump further apart as it opens. A woman enters. She's dressed like a Beggar in greasy jeans and a stained hoodie, with a frayed knit cap over her multicolored, dreadlocked hair. "Chief wants you."

Gerry doesn't follow when we leave the car. The farther away I walk, the fainter he feels. Samhain is waning. He'll be gone by midnight. I must bring Matthew to him by then. If I do, maybe he can rest in peace, despite being buried at the crossroads.

The woman leads us all the way back to the mail rail station where Helena and Gareth are waiting for us on the platform. Gareth's wearing a white lab jacket with a badge identifying him as a doctor at St. Mary's. A black, canvas medical bag is slung over his shoulder.

Helena taps and swipes at a tablet as she speaks. "Kensington Care Home is surrounded by our people. No one can enter or leave without us knowing. Gareth will accompany you. He can talk his way inside." She reaches into a pocket sewn into her glorious denim jacket skirt and pulls out two transit cards, which she hands to me and Lennon. "These will get you through our doors and also through station turnstiles." She nods toward our guard, who has unplugged the train and is now lifting the plexiglass shell over the cars. "Ruth will take you to the end of the line, beneath Lancaster Gate. It's a short walk from there to the care home."

Lennon's eyes widen. "Won't anyone notice we're on the tracks?"

Helena shakes her head. "This line has been closed and walled off for over fifty years. The train is battery-powered, so we're not on the grid. You both must swear on your honor not to tell anyone of this train's existence."

Something else to add to our growing list of things that

must never be known. Still, it's significant that Helena is allowing Lennon, the head of another clan, in on this secret. Maybe John Walks Long told her he's trustworthy. More likely, she loves my family enough to take a chance on him.

"On my honor," we say simultaneously.

"Gareth has a change of clothes for Matthew. Bring him down here after you've healed him."

I hug her because she's the best, just like I remember. When I was little, I wanted to be her, strong and heroic, dressed in fantastic, fabulous patches and rags.

She kisses my forehead. "Godspeed, Penny Sparrow." She spares a nod for Lennon.

He gives a wary nod back. This drives me crazy. We're all on the same side, right? Until we're not, I guess.

Ruth takes a seat behind the engine. We climb into the car behind her. Gareth secures the shell and sits across from me and Lennon. Thin cushions added to the shelf-like seats are the sole concession for comfort since this train was designed to carry mail, not people. The electric engine is silent, but the train makes its age known as it shakes, rattles, and squeaks its way down a slope and into the tube. The engine's front-mounted lantern is our only source of light, illuminating the track and narrow tunnel walls. We watch as the top of the shell almost scrapes the ceiling. A fan circulates air inside the car, but it's still stuffy and warm.

"Hope you're not claustrophobic," I say to Lennon, only half-joking.

He shakes his head before glancing all around the exterior. "Is it like this the whole way?"

"We'll pass through a couple of abandoned stations," says Gareth. "But otherwise, yeah."

"How long will it take?" I ask.

"About half-an-hour."

I suppress a groan. That's a long time to sit in awkward

silence, none of us able to speak our hearts or minds. I glance at Gareth's ID. "Do you really work at St. Mary's?"

He chuckles as he taps his badge. "It's fake. I have one for almost every hospital in London."

I know better than to ask why. "Are you still practicing?"

"Yeah. I'm still the clan's version of the National Health. Me, another former military doctor, and a few nurses, we can do most of what needs to get done. We even have a midwife."

Neither of us has anything to add to that. Small talk is hard when you have huge issues to discuss. I want so much to ask if he's seeing someone else. I hope he is. I want him to be happy. The melancholy in his eyes tells me he's not. Gerry was his first and last love, impossible to replace because there's no one like him. It'd be like me trying to replace Lennon. I don't want to think about that. Better to get down to business. I tell them about the layout of Kensington Care Home, and we discuss exit strategies in case things go south. Gareth reaches into his bag and pulls out two burner phones, which he hands to us.

"If we get separated," says Gareth, "don't try going through the tunnels yourselves. You'll get lost. Get on the underground at Paddington. Both lines will take you to St. James Park station. Call Helena - Maud - and she'll send someone to escort you to the Abode."

The mail train trundles past two dark, abandoned stations before going through a long tunnel that Gareth explains is beneath Hyde Park. The platform at the end of the line is dimly lit and shows signs of sparse habitation as if the Beggars only use this train for special circumstances. After climbing out, Ruth plugs the train into some kind of meter. I don't know the source of power and I know better than to ask. Gareth leads me and Lennon to an ancient lift that's more like a cage. Lennon and I eyeball the ceiling and each other as it creaks and groans the entire ride up. As it shudders to a stop, Gareth turns on his phone's flashlight and leads us through a dark, narrow corridor that's both stuffy and reeks of something dead.

"Are there rats?" I whisper.

"Yeah. We set traps," Gareth whispers back.

I shudder. "Do you empty them?"

"Me, personally? No."

I giggle, before choking back a memory of how funny he and Gerry were together.

We reach a door with a card reader. Gareth taps his phone and studies the screen. "We have access to the CCTV in the outer corridors. It's clear. Let's go."

He taps his transit card to the reader and opens the door. Then he takes us through a series of service corridors that lead to Paddington Station where we use our cards to get through the turnstiles. Outside, the restaurants are packed with the lunch crowd. We pass a curry house and the rich, spicy scent makes my mouth water. When was the last time I had a proper curry? I picture myself sitting in a restaurant with my family. We're laughing. Fighting over who gets the last pakora. Gareth is there. He and Gerry have an announcement. That's when they'd told us they'd be buying a caravan and joining us on the road. The happiness of the memory makes me almost smile until I glance at Gareth. Does he think of that, too, when he smells curry?

I swallow back these thoughts as we approach Kensington Care Home. A cold wind gusts through the square and tugs at the dying leaves on the trees, scattering them through the air. The sound makes me jump and I glance around like a spooked squirrel.

"Don't worry," says Gareth. "We have people positioned all over this square."

"The Two Dragon Clan has a lot of tricks…"

"So do we."

I exchange a look with Lennon. The Beggars might have

superior fire power, but they can't compete with the supernatural abilities of the Two Dragon Clan.

Inside the reception area, Gareth introduces himself as a doctor and us as visiting family members of Xavier Smith. I'm once again Emma Smith. Lennon signs in as Paul Smith. We take the lift to Matthew's ward. The nurses at the station barely glance at us as we walk past. It looks no different from when'd I'd been here before. We reach the end of the hall and I knock on Xavier Smith's door.

Auntie Enid answers and gasps with surprise, pressing her hand to her chest. "Penny, what are you doing here?" She looks past me at Lennon. "Is this… are you…?"

Lennon holds up his hand. He turns to Gareth. "We can't have you with us."

Gareth nods. "I'll stand guard out here."

"Great. Thanks."

Auntie Enid steps aside. Uncle Charles is beside Matthew's curtained bed. Did he just happen to be here? According to Bridie, his heart attack ruse was up and he'd gone back to regular work. It's more of a coincidence than I like.

Lennon stands a little taller as he says, "I'm here to heal your son."

"Dragon Son," both Matthew's parents give reverent bows.

I can't help asking, "Uncle Charles, why are you here?"

He gives me a narrow glare before harrumphing. "I'm spending my lunch hour with my son. Is that so odd?"

It's not and I feel a little ashamed, though I'm well justified in not trusting them.

"You have the Yin Pearl?" asks Lennon.

"Yes, but your wife…" Auntie Enid's eyes shift to me. "Have you and Penny…"

"No," we say at the same time.

Lennon continues. "You misunderstood Jade Dragon's

instructions. We don't need to be intimate to use the pearls together."

Her eyelids flutter. "But how else will you…"

"Jade Dragon has instructed me on how to proceed. It is not for you to question or to know any further mysteries of the pearls. That is reserved for the Dragon Son."

I smirk. Look at Lennon being a boss and owning the Wongs. Cool.

They bow again. Then Uncle Charles snatches his phone from his pocket. He glances at the screen. "This is about a patient. I have to take it. Please, don't proceed until I get back. I've reserved the room across the way and it's empty."

Lennon nods and Charles leaves the room.

"Want to meet Matthew?" I ask.

Lennon nods. We go to the bed and I gaze on the man lying there. I remember shaking him awake when I was a child. He'd never get angry. He'd blink his eyes to wakefulness and smile and call me Penny Lane, and let me and Kai drag him from bed to play a game or sing a song. I want that now, to shake him awake and hear him sing.

And hear him say what actually happened to my father.

Matthew

I can't wake up. The harder I tried, the worse it got. Imagine being trapped underwater and trying desperately to swim to the surface. You almost get there and something grabs hold of your feet and won't let go. Your arms flail. You kick against something that feel like concrete. The more you fight, the deeper you sink back in. So, you let go. You float up toward a bright light. It's warm and gives you the energy and oxygen to exist there, just below the surface.

Images waver and blur. Words smear like Vaseline. I can open my mouth to eat and drink. I know I'm being asked questions and even pleaded with, but I can't respond. When I try, I sink.

For a while, I sensed Gerry reaching out to me on the other side of a thick veil. I tried reaching back, but the bright light wouldn't allow it. Then he faded away, and I realized he was dead. I envied him. That had to be better than this half-life.

I can sense my parents tending me, their hands sometimes gentle, but often not. They're impatient. They want this done. But my family, my true family, is gone. My life is no life. I would leave it, sink a final time, but I can't. Not until I know what happened to them.

So, I live in my dreams. Whole lifetimes spent in my mind, wandering through the possibilities. I relive the day I first met Bridie and Gerry. I was like a moth drawn to the flame of her. Long red hair, bright green eyes, long bare legs. She played the violin with a passion I felt in my soul. The pub had accidentally double-booked us. I didn't care even though I had maybe 5 quid to my name. I was happy to sit there and watch her. Then her husband, with his black hair, blue eyes, and easy smile approached me and called me mate. Offered to split the stage time with me and the till. That was generous, given there were three of us. He was generous. Bought me a pint before we went on stage. When we jammed, it was like magic played through our fingers. The punters cheered and demanded more. The pub owner was pleased and asked the three of us to return the following week. A regular gig is like gold, so we agreed.

After he walked away, Gerry said, "You're a Sharper, yeah? Two Dragon Clan."

My shoulders tensed. "How did you know?"

"We're Strowlers." He lowered his voice dramatically. "Gypsies have a way of knowing these things." He winked.

"Oh, bugger off, Gerry," Bridie gave him a little shove. "He's taking the piss." Her soft, cold fingers tap my chest where my shirt has come unbuttoned, revealing the blue dragon tattooed over my heart.

We all laughed and ordered another round, and for the first time ever, I felt like I was among friends. When they found out I lived in a squat, they invited me to spend the night in their caravan. Of course, I said yes. They'd arrived on Vespas and Gerry's was loaded with their gear, so I climbed on behind Bridie. I tried not to cling to her lovely curves even though I'd never been on a scooter before. She had the most delicious smell, like vanilla, milk, and honey. Riding through the streets on that summer night, laughing, drinking in the big ugly city, and feeling freer than I'd ever had before, I think that's when I fell in love with her.

When we got to the encampment, they retrieved their baby daughter, Penny, from her sitter. She cuddled against her father, resting her sleepy head in the crook of his neck. A wild jealousy coiled up within me. I wanted Gerry's life with his sweet little girl and gorgeous wife and snug, warm caravan with a safe place to park it. He and I sat at the kitchen table while Bridie settled on the couch with a weary sigh. Penny cooed and squealed until her mother unbuttoned her top and popped out a gorgeous, engorged, pink and white breast. So that's where that heavenly scent came from.

I stared. I couldn't help it. Then I looked away as heat filled my face.

"Oy, love," Gerry said to Bridie as he nodded toward me.

Bridie looked up, saw my face, and flashed an embarrassed smile. "Sorry." She lifted her child, still attached to her breast, and headed for the bedroom in the back of the caravan.

I stammered apologies, which Gerry waved away. "Strowlers. We're expected to be virgins when we marry, but we're not at all modest."

I didn't have a clue what to think or say about that.

Gerry opened the fridge and took out two beers. We sat at the table and clicked bottles. Then Gerry said, "There's something you should know, mate. I'm gay."

The beer burned down my throat. I sputtered and coughed. No one admits to being gay on the Crossroads, and never to a stranger. "Why are you telling me this?"

"You're a Sharper. I don't want my gayness to taint you. Unless you don't care." He sipped his beer, his eyes on my face.

I took another sip. It burned less. "But you're married with a kid."

He shrugged. "I was trying to walk the Glory Road and do the right thing, yeah? And I love Bridie. I love her and my girl. They're everything. But I couldn't keep faking them. They deserved the truth. Bridie stayed with me rather than return to her parents. I keep up the sham for their sake. I won't leave them. Truth is, I don't know why I'm telling you. I like you." His eyebrows raised as I froze. "Not in that way, ya daft bugger. You were brilliant up there on stage. I'd like to gig with you, but I don't want to fake you out. There it is."

I liked Gerry, too. And Bridie. I wanted to keep gigging with them. Leaving family and clan to walk the Wayward Way was my statement that I wouldn't live by their rules or accept their customs. Here was my chance to prove it.

So, I told Gerry I didn't care, because I really didn't. In the back of my mind, a seed was planted: Bridie was available. More than that, though, I wanted to be with them, part of a family, no longer alone in my disgrace. So, I joined them, joined their band, Wild Sky, and joined my heart and fate to theirs. I would say Bridie fell into my arms, but that wasn't the case. I fell into hers and never left. Caution didn't exist for us, not even after she conceived Kai. She loved playing the woman with two husbands. Our children were happy with two fathers. Gerry hid behind that sham until he realized he wanted more, and we supported him.

In my dreams, Gerry and Gareth buy their own caravan with the money my parents give us for retrieving the Yin Pearl. Our lives go on as they did. Bridie conceives another child. We continue our walk on the Wayward Way, scandalizing those on the Glory Road and not give a damn. The children grow older and leave us to start families of their own. Sometimes, we approve of their choices, and other times we don't. Endless possibilities, this life I lost.

I have nightmares. Bad. Bridie and the children, murdered for our folly. These shake me and I sink deep into the watery murk until I can't take another breath. Somehow, that light pierces through the darkness and I concentrate on it. Allow it to envelope me so I can float to the near surface and dream again.

Then, one day, bored and restless, I reach for that light and pull myself up and out. I stand. For a glorious moment, I believe I've done it, that I'm healed, until I look in the mirror and see through myself to the bed where my body still lay. I don't panic because I can't. I have no physical sensations. A silvery, glowing cord tethers me to my body, so I decide to test its limits. I go to the door and reach for the handle, but my hand goes right through it. With a little push, my body follows and I'm in the care home's corridor. I look down. How am I not sinking through the floor? Then I realize I'm not standing or walking, I'm floating. Without the illusion of legs, it takes some effort before I can urge my presence down the hall toward the nurses' station. When I get there, I see them talk, but I can't hear anything. In this state, all senses are denied me except sight. Is this what it is to be a ghost? Even without a body, the thought terrifies me. I return to my room and retreat into my body, determined more than ever to survive.

Despite this fear, I try again the next time my parents come visit me. I glance at Father's paperwork and peer into Mother's purse, hoping for some glimpse of what might've become of my family. When they leave, I go with them, down the lift, to the carpark, and into their car. As we drive away, the silver cord tugs and I'm pulled through the car and into the street. Cars drive through me. I don't feel it, but it's still frightening, and I retreat to the sidewalk. My fear disappears when I realize I'm outside. I can't smell the air or feel the breeze, but I can look at the sky and even stare at the sun without blinking. I'm surrounded by people, by life instead of death, and I want to stay and explore, and be part of the world again.

I have no feeling except for my attachment to the cord and

it's wavering. Something tells me that if I don't return to my body soon, the cord will dissolve. Would that be so bad? At least in this state, I'm free of that room and bed, and useless body. I can search for my family now. If I find them, though, what will I do? They won't see me or have any sense of me. Could I bear seeing them again and not being able to embrace them?

No. I let go and allow the cord to draw me back into my body. As physical sensation returns, I realize I'm exhausted and I sleep for a long time.

After that, I'm more cautious as I leave my body and test the limits of the connection. I go out to the small park nearby and watch people eat lunch, feed birds, kiss and quarrel, and sleep rough on the iron benches. I get a sense of how much time has passed and try not to despair.

A new patient is placed in the room across from mine. It's my father. I hover near his bed as the doctor examines him. Neither he nor my parents look too concerned. As soon as the doctor leaves, my father gets out of bed and mother pulls out her phone. They speak as if making plans before my mother makes each call. What are they doing? They've cared for me all this time and I want to believe they have good intentions, but I don't trust them. I never have.

Time passes. My father leaves the room as if he's recovered and goes back to work. Mother carries a briefcase into my room, which is unusual. She never stays long enough to read or work. I follow her to the lobby and there they are, my family.

Joy overwhelms me and try hugging them, but my arms pass through them. I have so many questions. Why haven't they come to see me before now? Maybe not much time has passed. But when I look at my children, they're older and taller. Years have passed. Bridie's face has thinned and her eyes are haunted. I witness their shock and anger when they see my body. My parents have kept me hidden from them. Why?

Mother shows them pictures of our clan treasures, but for what purpose? I follow my family through the park to a nearby hotel, but my tether reaches its limit before I reach the front entrance. Why are they staying in a hotel? None of this makes any sense.

I return to my body so I can at least feel their gentle, loving hands, and their kisses and tears. I can even smell them though sight and sound remain a watery blur. Each time they visit, I feel stronger, like I'll break through the surface at any moment. And then they're gone.

Gone.

Were they even here? No. None of it was real. All of it is part of the never-ending void.

I sink.

I wait.

I dream.

Penny

"I told the nurses I'll be examining Mr. Smith and I'm not to be disturbed," says Uncle Charles when he returns. He notes Matthew's vital signs before removing the cords and tubes with a brusque efficiency. Maybe he has to detach himself in order to be an effective doctor, but I don't see any love in his actions. He wants this over with. Auntie Enid has a similar gleam in her eyes as she helps her husband, tugging at her son rather than easing him up.

That's when it hits me. This isn't about Matthew. It never has been. They'd found the Yin Pearl, but instead of receiving acclaim, they were robbed and shunned, and the son who'd risked his life to help them became a burden. Now, they believe they're finally going to get their just reward, and healing Matthew is nothing but a means to that end.

Lennon watches them with a squint and frown. It's not just me judging them harshly. He sees it, too. With a mutual nod, we hurry over to relieve them of their burdensome son. If I were Bridie, I know Auntie Enid would brush me away, but since I'm not, she allows me to take over. Matthew had physical therapy sessions while I was here before, so I know he can sit up on his own and do simple things like lift his legs and stretch out his arms. He can even stand and walk with assistance. It's as if his body knows what to do while his mind, his conscious self, remains trapped by his injury.

Lennon and I lead Matthew to a chair and adjust his body, so he's comfortably seated. I undo his hospital gown, exposing his bare back. His parents take hold of each other's hands in a tight squeeze. I want to believe its hope for their son and not their ambition.

I take a deep breath before tugging the red silk cord from around Matthew's neck. It holds a small, polished wood gourd painted with a yin-yang symbol. "The Yin Pearl is inside here. Does that matter?"

Lennon shakes his head.

As I place the cord around my neck, I feel the weirdest sensation, like the tiny pinprick of pain in my chest is a magnet attaching the pearl to that spot. It becomes a burning ember as energy pours from the pearl and courses through my body, joining the dragon energy already there. Part of me wants to fling off the pearl and run from the room. The other part of me feels powerful, like I can do anything, so no one better mess with me or come between what I want.

Lennon's mind touches mine. *Are you all right?*

Yeah. A little scared.

Me, too, but don't worry. We got this. I feel rather than see his smile, meant only for me.

I know.

You ready?

So ready. Let's do the thing.

I raise my right palm and Lennon presses his left palm against it. Our hands remain flat with a light pressure between us. Then we press our other palms to Matthew's back. I close my eyes and focus on the energy coursing between us. The pressure between our palms increases and the flow intensifies.

I lose all sense of myself as I feel Lennon, really feel him, as if I've lived his life. All his intense emotions flow into me. He hates more than he loves. The hatred he feels for Auntie Sylvia, Uncle George, Head Elder, and especially his father dominates his existence. It eats at his soul like acid and the only thing holding it back is the love he has for Tony and me. He loves others, his mother, Aaron, and Auntie Cat, and even Jade Dragon in a weird way, but the love that saves him comes from us.

Do I hate more than I love? I'm sure I do, just as I'm sure Lennon's love saves me. Hatred can't heal Matthew, so I concentrate on the love. I feel him do the same. The feelings intensify and become one, flowing through our palms and into Matthew.

I can feel it, mending neurons and synapses, healing scar tissue, strengthening atrophied muscles and tendons. Matthew opens his mouth and energy flows out of him in a mist. It dissipates, leaving behind a faint, bitter scent of illness and decay. The surge between Lennon and me trickles to nothing. The glow fades away. Dizziness overcomes me. We cling to each other to remain standing.

"You all right?" he whispers.

I don't know. The energy is gone. Or is it? I still feel something deep inside, a part of Lennon that will never leave. No wonder they required the users of the Yin and Yang Pearls be married. The Dragon Touch creates an intimacy so intense, it binds you to the other person.

Matthew raises his head as he sits up. He glances around with clear eyes that blink rapidly. He scrubs his face and twists around to stare at me. "Penny?"

Tears fill my eyes. I smile so hard I think my face will break. I reach out to embrace him, but before I can, his parents are there.

They hold him and pat his back and weep. I can't begrudge

them this, so I step back. He embraces them, too, but his eyes are bewildered. Then his expression changes, becoming wary. He pulls away and stares at them. He speaks in a raspy, rusty voice. "You kept me here."

His parents step back as they exchange looks. Their joy shifts into something else. Auntie Enid lifts her chin. "Yes, Son, we kept you here, safe from those who would harm you."

"The pearl. You wanted the pearl."

"We gave it to you, to keep you alive."

Matthew looks at his father. "Gerry?"

Uncle Charles shakes his head. "He was already dead. There was nothing I could do."

Matthew shakes his head fiercely. He doesn't believe his father any more than I do. He comes to his feet with an unsteady but surprising ease.

"Take it easy, Son. I need to examine you."

He waves his father away and turns to me, arms wide open. "Penny Lane."

My heart explodes. This is real. Matthew is alive. This is his hug, strong and gentle, like him. The healing power of the pearls extended throughout his body, returning mass and strength to his atrophied tendons and muscles.

He strokes my hair as my shoulders shake and tears soak into his hospital gown. Then he lifts my head so he can gaze into my eyes and whispers, "Penny, how old are you?"

I swallow hard to contain my emotions. This is a moment of hard truth for him. "Eighteen."

He whispers the number as he sinks back into his chair. Then he says aloud. "Three years." He looks up at me with sad, lost eyes. "Bridie and Kai? Where are they?"

And a hard truth for me. "San Francisco."

His brow wrinkles. Auntie Enid pipes up, "Bridie remarried. She and the children moved there with her new husband."

Matthew's face goes blank with shock. I want to shove her into the wall. "Tell him why she remarried."

She gives a callous shrug. "To keep you safe, Son, we had to fake your death. Even Bridie and the children thought you were dead. But let me tell you that little cow wasted no time in finding herself another man."

"She's lying," I snap back.

Matthew looks at his parents. "You told Bridie and the children I was dead?"

"We had to," says Uncle Charles. "We had no choice."

Matthew turns back to me. "But you were here. I remember you being here, all of you." He rubs his forehead. "Only once. Then you disappeared, and I thought I'd imagined it."

So, he wasn't entirely out of it. That means he knows his parents' motives aren't pure. "We were here last week. Your parents finally told us what had happened to you."

"Why? What changed?"

"There's a new Dragon Son." I reach for Lennon's hand. We share a smile because this is the moment when everything we've gone through becomes worthwhile. "We used the Yin and Yang Pearls to heal you."

Matthew stares at our clasped hands as if I'm holding a poisonous snake. He shows no gratitude as he eyes Lennon. "You're Michael Lau's son?"

Lennon's smile evaporates. "Yeah."

"Where's your father? Dead?"

"Yeah."

Matthew exhales but otherwise shows no relief. "Penny, are you married to this boy or…?"

I sigh. Worrying about my virtue even now? I thought he of all people would get it. I squeeze Lennon's hand before letting go. "No, we're not married or whatever you're thinking. Lennon's my best friend."

Matthew stares at me with stricken eyes and whispers, "Penny, no. No."

"Son," interrupts Charles. "We swore an oath not to speak of what happened that night."

"You swore an oath, not me. Penny needs to know the truth." Matthew juts his chin at Lennon. "His father killed Gerry."

Matthew

Family is my weakness whether it's that of my birth or that of my heart. I walked away from my birth family to be with my heart family and I have no regrets. When Mother called me in a panic, telling me she and Father had lost the Yin Pearl and asking me for help, I told her no.

Gerry was nearby when I got the call. Mother and I spoke in Cantonese, but he's a Strowler. Their eyes and ears are trained to read expression and emotion. As soon as I hung up, he asked, "What's up?"

I told him because those same keen senses would know a lie and because I trusted him with my life. To be honest, I was hoping we could figure out a way to help my parents. I needed him, like always.

I was raised to be a scholar, not a warrior, and had no practical experience when I dropped out of Oxford to be a wandering minstrel on the Wayward Way. Such defiance. So poetic. So stupid. I was half-starved and near ready to crawl back to my birth family when Bridie and Gerry took me in.

We made our living by playing in pubs and busking on the street, but that wasn't enough, not for three adults and two children. To supplement our income, Bridie told fortunes and Gerry ran shell games and picked pockets. I felt useless and wanted to contribute more, so I offered to teach him the Two Dragon Clan's Stealth Skills in exchange for teaching me the Strowlers' art of thievery.

We excelled in our new skills and abandoned petty larceny to take up a more dangerous game, retrieving stolen objects. Our clients were victims who knew the perpetrator and didn't want the police involved. We could have had a thriving business if we did only that, but we were musicians first and didn't want to chance leaving Bridie and the kids on their own if we got caught or killed, so we only went out on necessity and for the big-ticket items.

This time was different. Not a pawnshop or a private home, but the Two Dragon Clan *kongsi*. My parents wanted Gerry, not me, and promised him a lorry load of money, enough to pay in full the caravan he and Gareth had been eyeing, so he agreed. I refused to let him go without me, reminding them I'd been inside the *kongsi* and knew the layout. My parents' desperation was such that they relented. Father had a friend on the inside who'd offered to help. The friend said he could provide an open door and the location of the pearl. The rest would be up to us.

Chinatown is close to Piccadilly Circus, which is always a madhouse. That night, it was packed with drunken football fans picking fights with each other. We waited in a nearby restaurant until Father got a text from his friend giving us the exact time the *kongsi's* alley door would be unlocked, unguarded, and unmonitored. This would only last a few seconds, so we needed to be there. The friend instructed Father to create a distraction at the front entrance and gave directions on how to find the pearl, but there was a problem. There were two pearls, and we needed to steal both. That made us suspicious, but Father promised he would return both pearls to the clan. How that happened wasn't our concern.

I wanted to walk away, but with a twinkle in his eye, Gerry doubled the price, and Father agreed. I tried arguing with Gerry, but he wouldn't hear it. That kind of money would see us through an entire year. How could we walk away from that?

At the given time, Father went to the front door of the *kongsi* and pounded on it, claiming to be chased by hooligans, and pleading for help. Meanwhile, Gerry and I used the Shadow Skill to slip into the back entrance.

The building seemed eerily empty. Racing up the stairs, we passed no one on the first floor. On the second floor, there were guards standing outside a closed door. Maybe some kind of meeting? I couldn't believe we were that lucky, so I didn't. Something was up and we needed to get over and out, fast. We stopped just below the third-floor landing and I peered around the corner. A single guard stood in front of the third door to the left, just as described in the friend's text. Gerry and I didn't have to talk. We'd worked this sham before, easy as you please. It's called "Comes a Cove." Whichever of us looks most out-of-place comes wandering out in full sight, looking confused.

Gerry strolled out the staircase and came down the hall, waving to the guard. "Oy, mate. I'm here about the furnace. They said you could help me, yeah?"

The startled guard held up his hand but didn't reach his weapon. "Who told you to come up here?"

"Dunno. Some bloke downstairs called someone and then said to go upstairs." He pointed to a door at the end of the hall as he sauntered past the guard. "That the furnace?"

"Hold on. No one called me about this."

As the guard turned his back to follow Gerry, I was on top of him. Using *dim mak,* I jabbed a pressure point at his neck and knocked him unconscious. A quick pat down gave us the card we needed to gain entrance. We dragged him in with us and closed the door. The room was windowless, tight with filing cabinets and small enough we had to step over the guard to move around. The wall safe was open and there, lying on a black cloth, were the two pearls. One had a greenish glow while the other was more yellowish.

We looked at each other, shrugged, and each grabbed one pearl. I got the yellowish one. Then something, or rather someone, brushed my mind. It was my father. We hadn't shared the Silent Speech in years, not since I was a child, because I hadn't trusted him since then. My first instinct was to push away, but I could sense his urgency, so I let him in.

They know. Get out now.

Shit.

I told Gerry. He looked at his pearl and said, "Let's not get caught red-handed." He swallowed it and winked. "It'll all come out in the end."

I swallowed mine, too, and sent a quick prayer to Jade Dragon that the pearls wouldn't harm us.

We hurried out the door to an empty corridor but heard feet pounding up the stairs. We rushed to the furthest room and locked the door behind us. I yanked open the single window and looked down to the alley below. An easy fall for me. Harder, since I'd be taking Gerry, but we could still do it. I turned to him and he was on his knees, choking, his face bright red and tears streaming down his cheeks.

Shitshitshit.

I lifted him up and performed the Heimlich maneuver. The pearl shot out of his mouth, hit the wall, and rolled under a cabinet. Gerry broke free from me and scrambled after it, still coughing. I grabbed him and yanked him up.

The door crashed open and there stood Michael Lau, the Dragon Son, surrounded by armed men. He stared at us with eyes that contained death no matter what we said or did. He lifted his hand, and I knew what that meant.

I wrapped my arms around Gerry and made a mad dash for the window.

The Dragon Shout hit Gerry full in the chest. He recoiled into me as I launched out the window. Guns fired. A bullet clipped my shoulder, damaging my *chi* so I couldn't attempt the Flying Skill. As we fell, Gerry twisted around so that when we hit the ground, he took all the impact. Almost all. We landed in the alley on top of a grate, but I bounced off Gerry and my head hit the road.

Nothing. I'm dead.

But I'm not.

A soft, yellowish glow held me together. Eventually, I found myself floating beneath the surface of consciousness where I waited and wondered and reached for that light.

Lennon

My dad killed Penny's dad.

Of course, he did.

I thought it couldn't get worse, that he'd ruined me and Tony, our family and our clan, but no. He had to ruin Penny's life, too. Not to mention Bridie, Kai, Matthew, his parents, Gareth… I doubt I can name everyone.

I'm starting to feel sympathy for Head Elder and Uncle George. I thought they hated him because they're evil and he was righteous and good, and they envied his power, but he was evil, too. Evil enough to fuck his sister-in-law and deny their child. Evil enough to kill someone over a fucking magic pearl.

I thought I hated him before, but now hatred fills my gut with bile, burning all the way up to my throat.

Penny and Matthew won't look at me. Does she hate me? How can she not? I've lost her. My heart pounds so hard, I'm dizzy. I should say something, but what?

"I'm sorry," I croak out, like that will help anything. They turn toward me, and I look away, so I won't see their anger and contempt.

"It's not your fault," Penny whispers.

No, but I'm tainted with my father's actions. All his bad choices have landed on my shoulders like a boulder, crushing me under its weight. I want to run away so I don't have to face them, but that's what I always do, and it doesn't make things any better. Head Elder and Uncle George will still be after them. I have to see this through to the bitter end.

Her mind brushes mine. We don't speak. I know she can feel what I'm feeling. I let down my barrier so I can feel her, too. Sorrow, worry, anger, even hatred, but not aimed at me. Not yet, anyway. Will she feel the same tomorrow after she's had time to think about it? How can we stay together if every time she looks at me, she sees the son of her father's killer? How does love survive that?

She turns to Matthew's parents. "That's not the story you told us."

They exchange quick glances before Enid snaps, "What are you talking about?"

"When my family was here, you didn't tell us about Uncle Charles' friend."

"Of course not," says Charles. "I swore to keep his identity secret."

"But Auntie Enid said she gave directions to Gerry and Matthew."

"To keep his identity secret," he repeats through clenched teeth.

"And you didn't tell us there were two pearls."

"We swore secrecy about all these things," says Enid.

"Including that Michael Lau killed Gerry?"

Her eyes shift to her son before she says, "Of course not. We didn't know. Otherwise, we'd have never sent your family to San Francisco."

"Wait." Matthew holds up his hand. He squints at his parents. "You sent Bridie and the children to San Francisco?"

While the Wongs stammer through their half-ass excuses, Penny touches my mind. *They're lying.*

For sure.

Do you remember your dad coming here three years ago?

No. Dad went on lots of secret trips. I'd wake up in the morning and he'd be gone. No explanation. Same with Uncle George.

Are you thinking what I'm thinking?

Definitely.

I turn to Charles. "Was your friend my uncle, George Lau?"

He doesn't blink, but he licks his lips before saying, "I swore an oath not to reveal his identity."

There it is. Dad must have found out that the Wongs had the Yin Pearl and ordered it stolen before Head Elder could get his hands on it. Uncle George saw an opportunity and stole both it and the Wisdom Pearl. He somehow got lucky and found the Wisdom Pearl after Gerry spit it out. I do the calendar math and it adds up. About a month later, he was caught taking photos in the Chisel Knife Mountain caverns. He'd been trying to figure out how to use the Wisdom Pearl.

"Father," says Matthew abruptly. "Was that George Lau? Was there something going on that you didn't tell me about?"

"This isn't the time to discuss such things," interrupts Enid. "Your father needs to examine you."

"I feel fine," says Matthew. He stares at his arms and legs, flexing them as if astounded they belong to him. "How is this possible? I shouldn't even be able to stand after being in a coma for so long."

"Penny and the Dragon Son are young," she replies. "The youthful nature of their *chi* must have restorative powers."

"I still need to examine you," says his father. He looks at me and Penny. "All of you. You both expended a significant amount of *chi*. You must be exhausted."

Except I'm not. We expelled dragon energy healing

Matthew, so I feel more normal now. I can't tell him that, so I shrug. "Yeah, okay."

"All right," says Matthew. "But then we talk. I need answers."

Charles turns to me and Penny. "You can wait in the room across the hall. Lay down and rest. You need to replenish your *chi*."

Penny nods, but then turns to Matthew, laying her hand on his arm. "Gareth is outside."

"Gareth?" He blinks rapidly. "What's he doing here?"

"We saw Helena before we came here. The Beggar Clan are guarding us."

"Gareth," he whispers again before nodding.

Penny opens the door and leans her head out. Gareth steps inside and his blue eyes widen with shock at the sight of Matthew.

"I can't believe it. How?" As he speaks, he and Matthew embrace. "Ah, god, you're alive. It's a bloody miracle." He holds Matthew at arm's length. A forlorn hope lights his face. "Gerry. Is it possible?"

Matthew shakes his head. Tears fill his eyes, and Gareth's, and Penny's. And mine. Matthew's parents remain stone-faced. They're hiding something and they're going to tell me what that is. Dad might have been the one to kill Gerry, but I'm certain the person responsible is Uncle George.

Penny

Auntie Enid looks down the hall before leading into the room across the way. I frown as I glance around. This isn't right. The room is clean, even sanitized, with crisp, undisturbed bedding and unused water glasses wrapped in plastic. There are no suitcases or discarded coats, or any sign that anyone has been in here recently.

"I thought you and Uncle Charles were staying here," I say.

She blinks and flinches. "Well… well, yes, we… we… were," She clears her throat and that pinched look returns to her eyes. "Bridie misunderstood me, as usual. We spent one night here and then we moved."

"Where?"

"To… to… that hotel. That one you stayed at. Um… the one nearby."

"The Hyde Swan?"

She glares at me. "Of course."

I glance at Lennon and see the tilt of his head. He's only just met Enid, but he can already see through her bullshit.

She huffs impatiently. "I don't need your attitude, Penny. My son… he's back. He's returned to me. I can't think about anything else. Don't you dare question me like a common criminal. I swear, you're becoming more like your mother every day." She turns on her heel and skitters out of the room.

"You're welcome?" Lennon says to the door she shuts in our faces.

We exchange glances again, but without Enid there as a buffer, we quickly look away. I perch on the edge of the bed while Lennon folds into the only chair, his head bowed. We need to talk, but my throat is clogged. Pain and joy have intertwined and attached to my chest with suction cups, one draining my energy while the other feeds it back to me. I want to collapse onto the mattress, but I also want to jump up and down and scream. Instead, I reach out with the Silent Speech and brush Lennon's mind.

Anger. Sorrow. Hatred. Self-loathing. I have to weave through them all to reach him.

I'm so sorry, he says.

It's not your fault.

It doesn't matter. My father killed your father. He raises his head, a stark, pain-filled challenge in his eyes. *Can you look at me and not think about that?*

I can't. Gazing into those eyes, I picture how it went down. Gerry, cocky and ready for a fight, not seeing what Matthew saw. Not realizing until that bolt of dragon energy hit him square in the chest. Even falling out the window, his life draining out of him, he twisted his body to spare Matthew. That's my father, a hero. And that's Lennon's father, a murderer. Yes, they were stealing from him, but did he have to use deadly force?

I didn't realize I was thinking aloud until Lennon replies. *I knew he was a killer. I mean, I'd asked Mom if he'd ever killed anyone, and she wouldn't tell me, which meant yes. Since he was so righteous, I believed he only killed in self-defense. Turns out, he did what he wanted to get what he wanted and didn't care who suffered. Not me, not Tony, not your family.*

I really don't blame you.

Yeah, but… His long sigh deflates him. *When I look at Tony, I think about how his mother killed mine.*

Do you blame him?

No, of course not. But when he looks at me, I'm sure he thinks about how my dad ruined his life.

Does Tony blame you? No.

Tears shine from his eyes. *But I feel like I deserve it, for being the son Dad sheltered and used as a reason for his crimes.*

His crimes are not your fault. Ever. It will take time, but we'll get past this. I hope. I gnaw my lip at the gnawing truth within me. *I'm angry, but not just with your father. I'm mad at Gerry and Matthew, too, and his parents. It was too dangerous. The Wongs shouldn't have asked and my dads shouldn't have agreed.*

A hesitant look crosses his face.

What?

I don't want to make excuses, because my dad is totally guilty for what he did, but I think they were all set up by my uncle.

Yeah. I think so, too, which is why we need to move on. We have to work together to defeat your uncle or our families will never be safe.

He rubs his face and wipes his tears on his sleeves. My heart breaks a little more because I hate seeing him so hurt. Lennon is my best friend and I'll always love him, no matter what, even something as huge as this, but he's right. It will be a long time before I can look at him and not see the son of Gerry's killer. There's no way to get past that, but it doesn't change how I feel about him.

Are you tired? I ask.

His sad eyes look grateful at this change of topic. *Yeah. Are you?*

Yeah. I guess we have jet lag… Excuse me. Dragon lag.

His mouth quirks. Mine does, too. Even a tiny joke feels enormous.

He rubs his chest in the same spot where I still feel a pinprick of energy and pain. *I thought I used all the energy Jade Dragon gave me when we healed Matthew, but now I feel like some of it's still there, and always will be.*

Me, too. Which is kind of a scary thought, but I'm done with thinking for now. All the emotion passing between us has exhausted me. I can barely keep my eyes open. I tug off my shoes and roll onto the far side of bed. I take a quick breath before patting the space beside me.

His eyes widen. *Are you sure?*

My eyes narrow in a fake glare. *Would I offer if I wasn't?*

He knows I wouldn't because he knows me that well. He takes off his shoes and eases onto the space beside me. The hospital bed is wider than a normal single mattress, but it's still impossible to lie beside each other and not touch. Our hands brush before clasping tight. The pressure releases, but we don't let go. Our legs, hips, shoulders relax against each other as our heads rest on the same pillow. All I feel in this moment is love for him, so I close my eyes and allow myself to drift away before the other thoughts return.

I dream I'm on Jade Dragon's back again, in that strange, pressurized bubble that protects me from the elements. I'm alone, undulating above the ocean. I should be afraid, but I'm not, because this is where I belong.

Where are you taking me? I ask.

To where your journey ends and begins, he replies in that ancient voice that also somehow seems young.

What does that mean?

He doesn't answer. Lennon warned me he was an asshole that way.

We fly a while longer before he says, *Behold, where he abides and awaits.*

I don't ask who, because I know he means my ancestor, Master Stoorworm. There's nothing below us but vast, endless ocean. The waves foam and stir before forming a giant whirlpool. I feel its pressure and wonder if it will suck us in. The pinprick in my chest sharpens like a knife and burns like fire. A great dragon arises from the deep. He's dark green with eyes red as flame and is twice the size of Jade Dragon. Water streams off his scales and steam hisses through his snout. Fear turns my body into a quivering mass of jelly. I'd slide off if Jade Dragon wasn't holding me in place. Master Stoorworm eyes me with regal disdain. He has no trace of Jade Dragon's humanity, despite having lived as a man and coupling with a woman... no, a fairy. Still, he recognizes me, and I realize the dragon power remaining within me is from him, not Jade Dragon.

Master Stoorworm dives back into the ocean. The waves splash so high, they brush Jade Dragon's belly. I slide off as he undulates away. I'm falling...

I gasp. Something presses against my temple. It's cold and hard. My eyes blink open. Enid Wong is holding a gun to my head.

Penny

Uncle Charles stands at the foot of the bed, his gun aimed at Lennon. My heart gallops. I suck in air through my nostrils, my mouth clamped tight with shock.

Am I dreaming?

No. The cold, metallic press of the gun barrel against my head feels too real. Auntie Enid stares down at me with merciless eyes, seeing only the daughter of the woman she hates.

I squeeze Lennon's hand, hard. He stirs, his eyelids fluttering before popping wide open as he flinches back in surprise.

Uncle Charles follows his movement with his gun. "Don't move. Keep your mouth shut. If you try anything, Penny dies."

That pinprick in my chest still burns, but after that dream I realize it's not like fire. It's like ice. Dragon energy isn't hot, it's cold, logical, remorseless. I channel some of Master Stoorworm's frigid flame into Lennon and feel his fear and confusion melt away.

The Dragon Touch, he says. *Matthew's illness. Can we pass it to both of them?*

I search the Yin Pearl and find my answer. *No. Only one of them.*

Which one?

Enid reaches out with her free hand, her manicured nails scraping my neck as she grasps at the cord of the Yin Pearl. Despite her weapon, I recoil, lifting my shoulder to protect my neck. *Her. She's the stronger of the two.*

She steps back, her gun still aimed at me. "Don't fight me, Penny," she snaps. "I'll do what I have to do."

"We don't want to kill you," says Uncle Charles. "Give us the pearls and this will all be over."

Can I really do this to Matthew's mother? I can, but… I feel Lennon's *chi* coursing through me, but it's an uneven flow. The energy might be from dragons, but we're still human, distracted by conflicting emotions. We need more time. I have to stall them. I swallow to moisten my throat. My voice still comes out in a dry rattle. "Gareth. He'll stop you."

A grim, smug smile stretches Charles's mouth. "Gareth is with Matthew, catching up while I examine you. I told them it would be awhile. These guns have silencers. They won't hear a thing."

"He's Mad Maud's brother. We're under the Beggar Clan's protection."

Enid sneers. "The Beggar Clan is nothing compared to the Two Dragon Clan."

"Then why are you threatening the Dragon Son?"

Her sneer spreads to Lennon. "He's not the Dragon Son."

They support George. As if that's a big surprise. I only have one more shot. "Matthew will never forgive you for this. Neither will Kai."

Hesitation crosses their faces. They pause, long enough for me to center myself and allow our combined *chi* to flow through me and into the Yin Pearl. I search for Matthew's illness and find something else. A different type of power; one that takes rather than gives.

Enid's gun scrapes my scalp. "They will forgive us. Once we're reinstated in the clan and given a place of honor, they'll realize it was all done for them."

My heart pounds again. I suck in a breath. "Not if you kill us."

"Give us the pearls and we won't."

There's a tap on the door. Gareth. He's come to check on us. He'll save us. Or be killed by the Wongs if they get spooked. I use the distraction to reach out to Lennon. *I'm going to try something else.*

Something else? What do you mean?

No time. Just give me all you've got.

Charles backs away, his gun still trained on Lennon. He opens the door a crack, glances out, and steps aside. A man enters. He's Asian, middle-aged and dressed in dark, nondescript clothing. He stares at us, expressionless, then turns to George and speaks in Cantonese.

Lennon's energy flows through me and with it a sense of oneness. I think his thoughts, feel his emotions, and hear with his ears.

"Why are they still alive?" asks the man.

Charles licks his lips, his eyes shifting to me. "Only the boy needs to die, right? Not the girl."

"Both," says the man. "If you won't do it, I will."

"Hurry and get it over with," says Enid, grabbing hold of her husband's sleeve and tugging him out of the way.

The assassin reaches into his jacket pocket and pulls out a gun.

Our souls combine, as they did for the Dragon Touch, but instead of sending out healing energy, the Yin Pearl becomes a vacuum, sucking in the life essence of Charles, Enid, and the assassin. The Yang Pearl wraps them in an energy web, paralyzing their movement. Their startled faces grimace as they try to resist. The assassin uses his *chi* to fight back, pushing against our combined power as he raises his arm against the force, trying to fire his weapon. Lennon lifts his other hand and makes a tugging motion. All three guns fly from their hands and land on the bed between us. Lennon reaches out again and lifts the Wongs and the man in the air. They jerk like puppets on a string until I drain enough energy that they go limp and unconscious. I can suck in more, take it all, leave them lifeless husks as they would've left us. I can and I should. They're too dangerous to live.

I know, says Lennon. *I want that, too, but will Matthew and Kai forgive us?*

No. They won't. They're not worth that. Better to leave them alive to face their son with all their treachery and evil deeds revealed.

Lennon eases them to the ground, not out of kindness, but so they won't make any noise. The energy flow between us subsides. I close my eyes as a wave of dizziness passes through me. I shake it off. There's no time for weakness. We rise from the bed and stand over them, staring at their prone forms.

"Are you okay?" asks Lennon.

I shake my head. "I feel weird, like their energy is trapped inside the Yin Pearl."

"How did you know how to do that?"

Good question. I rub the pinprick in my chest. "It's like the knowledge was in the pearl and I found it."

"Yeah. Same here."

"You couldn't do that before?" I make a lifting motion.

"No."

I rub at the pinprick's icy burn. "You feel that?"

Lennon nods and rubs his chest, too. We share a look that says what we don't want to speak, either Silent or aloud. Jade Dragon changed us in some way and made us more... dragon-like. Would it last forever? I can't dwell on that now with so much going on. I pull out my phone and text Gareth.

> Come to our room. Bring Matthew. Watch out for any strangers.

Is something wrong?

> Yes.

Moments later, there's a tap on the door. I open it and let them in. Matthew is wearing the clothes Gareth brought him. They hang loose on his thin frame. He gasps and drops to his knees beside his parents. "What happened? Who did this?"

"We did," I say.

He covers his eyes as he grimaces. "What did they do?"

Gareth glances at the guns on the mattress before eying me cautiously. "Penny, love, what happened?"

I'm dizzy again and I plop down on the bed. Their life essence within the pearl… it needs to be absorbed or released.

"I'll tell them," says Lennon.

While he speaks, I close my eyes and center myself. This energy, it's not mine and I don't want it. I'm not sure if the Wongs can recover without it. Do I want to be responsible for their deaths? As much as I hate them, no.

When Lennon finishes speaking, Matthew turns to me. I nod and whisper. "It's true."

He stands. "I want to hear it from them. Can you…?"

I reach for Lennon's hand. As his power courses through me, I stretch out my free hand and release the life essence back into the fallen bodies. Conflict, anger, desperation, greed, determination, all these feelings and more flow out too fast for me to grasp at their meaning. It drains but also relieves me, and Lennon's energy renews my strength. When it's all gone, I shudder with relief I'm done with them.

The Wongs and the assassin twitch and moan before staring up at us with startled eyes. Gareth grabs and points one of the guns at them. As the assassin rises to his knees, Gareth presses the business end to his forehead.

"Son," says Enid as she and Charles try to rise.

"No, stay where you are." Matthew grabs another gun off the mattress and holds it on them.

They remain kneeling, their eyes shifting as they survey their situation. Charles licks his lips. "I don't know what Penny and this boy told you…"

"They told me what happened."

"And you believed them?" Enid struggles to make her shaking voice authoritarian. "We are your parents. We're the ones who kept you safe for three years. Three years. Do you know how hard that was? Do you have any idea how much it cost, keeping you here in a private facility, with your identity hidden? This is how you repay us, by questioning our motives?"

Matthew draws in a shaking breath. "Mother, I'm not blind. I know what I'm seeing right now. If you've ever cared for me, you'll tell me the truth."

"We had no choice," she wails before covering her mouth with her hand.

A look of resignation comes over Charles's face as he speaks. "We were desperate after the Yin Pearl was stolen from us, so I called George Lau, a fellow scholar, and asked him to talk to his brother. He told me the situation was complicated and our only hope was to retrieve the pearl, and he would help. He came to London and set everything up so Matthew and Gerry could sneak inside the *kongsi*, but it all went wrong. He went into a rage, blaming us for losing the pearl. Head Elder cast us out of the clan. We were afraid to tell anyone when we found it again, fearful it would be taken while leaving us in disgrace. We had no plan beyond sending Kai to

San Francisco to befriend the Dragon Son's heir. Then, last week, after Penny and her family left, George Lau arrived. He told us everything, explained how it was his evil brother's fault, and persuaded us to admit that Matthew had the pearl. He said he would help us. All we had to do was lure that boy here, but he and Penny came unexpected."

Lennon and I exchange glances. George must've used the Wisdom Pearl to persuade them to his side. Even so, they stayed on his side after he left and the effect of the pearl diminished.

"Son." Charles tries standing again, but Gareth's gun convinces him otherwise. He gapes and glares before gathering his dignity with a harrumph. Then he jerks his head at Lennon. "That boy isn't the Dragon Son. Neither was his father. George Lau told us everything. He is the true Dragon Son and he'll restore us to our place in the clan."

Matthew clutches his hair. "I don't give a fuck who the bloody Dragon Son is. You tried to kill my daughter."

"She's not your daughter," snaps Enid. "That woman was never your wife." She glances at the gun in Matthew's hand and her eyes go sly. "If you side with us, we can return to our clan. All of us. You and Kai as well." She turns to the assassin beside her. "Isn't that right?"

The man nods. "You weren't the target. My master, the true Dragon Son, only wants the boy dead."

"You said you came to kill us both," says Lennon.

The assassin doesn't deny it or acknowledge Lennon at all.

"He's lying. We'd never harm Penny." Charles looks down as he speaks.

Enid doesn't. "Son, you belong with us and your clan."

Tears fill Matthew's eyes. How could they do this to him? He's only just recovered. Don't they understand how fragile he is? Then his slumped shoulders straighten and wipes his face as a glint of ice comes to his eyes. The Yin Pearl kept him alive for three years. The Yang Pearl brought him back to life. Dragon energy course through his veins and allows him to stare down at his parents without mercy.

"No, I don't. I never have and I never will." He turns to Lennon. "Dragon Son, I know you can't forgive them, but can you spare them?"

Lennon looks down at the Wong with a similar icy stare. They flinch and turn to their son with mute, pleading eyes. Lennon sucks in a breath. "For the sake of your son and grandson, I'll let you go, but you are banished from the clan forever. I take no responsibility for any action taken against you if you continue to support George Lau."

The Wongs show no gratitude or submission beyond their bowed heads. I know they'll call their master the moment we're gone.

"What about him?" asks Gareth, his gun pressed against the assassin's temple. Despite his bravado, I see the hesitation in his eyes. He's a doctor. Killing doesn't come easy to him and he shouldn't be in the position to rid us of our enemies.

I reach out to Lennon. *Matthew's illness is trapped in the pearl. I can't heal anyone else until I release it.*

Let's do it.

What about the whole karma thing? Will it bite us in the ass?

He came to kill us and the moment we turn our backs, he'll try again, so, karma's good.

More like on the gray side of good enough, but I'll take it. Our palms press together. The assassin cringes as he realizes something is about to happen. Before he can react further, I reach into the pearl and using our joined energy, pour Matthew's illness into him. Guttural groans escape from his throat and his eyes roll up before he collapses, unconscious.

Gareth kneels beside him to check his pulse. "What the devil have you done?" he asks, looking at me like I'm a stranger.

Lennon answers. "He's in a coma. Matthew's coma. We transferred it to him."

Enid and Charles cower and stare at us with terrified eyes as if certain they're next. Matthew… I'm afraid to look at him. Does he think I'm a monster now? I clench my teeth before glancing at him.

He's rubbing his forehead. Too much has happened in such a short time. He must be freaking out on the inside. Then he closes his eyes and takes a deep breath. When they reopen, I see the glint of dragon fire. He, like Lennon and me, can still tap into the cold logic of Jade Dragon's energy. Hopefully, it will last long enough for him to adjust to his new world.

"How are you two doing all this?" asks Gareth. "Where did the power come from?"

"From a dragon," replies Matthew.

Gareth sputters, but his face sobers as he realizes Matthew is serious. "We'll talk about it in the Abode. We have to leave now."

I'm not sure how we're going to talk about it anywhere but leaving it for later sounds good to me.

As we head for the door, Charles stutters, "What… what about him?" He nods at the prone assassin.

Gareth's face goes stone cold. He's a doctor, but he's also a soldier in the army that is the Beggar Clan. "What about him? He's your mess to clean up." He turns to Matthew and his eyes soften with concern. "You okay?"

Matthew takes a deep breath and nods. "Let's get out of here."

His parents reach out, their faces contorted. Enid pleads, "Son, son. Please. Don't leave us like this."

Lennon opens the door and looks down the hall. He nods and we step out. Matthew is the last to leave, and he closes the door without looking back.

Lennon

We leave through the lobby without stopping at the front desk. Matthew walks in our midst, wearing sunglasses and a hoodie, and looking sketchy as hell. A receptionist looks up, but we're through the door before she can speak.

It's still cold outside, but the clouds have cleared and there's a light breeze. At the bottom of the stairs, Matthew stops and lifts his face, shading his eyes as he blinks in the sunlight. He takes a deep breath and whispers, "It's been so long."

Penny watches him with a painful smile, like her heart is about to burst. Her eyes are sad, but also so happy that it feels worth every second of every minute of everything shitty that's happened to me.

Matthew doesn't move, so we linger, allowing him to have his moment. After three years stuck in bed with only his trash fire parents for company, I'm surprised he's not crazy or maybe he was and we healed him of that, too. Still, all those years surviving on the power of the Yin Pearl have to have done something to him, changed him in some way.

Across the square, a large group of tourists are milling

around in front of a hotel. Tour guides hold up signs written in Korean. The collective sound of their excited voices echoes off the walls, giving me a claustrophobic feeling. An enclosed area like this isn't safe. We need to get a move on. I'm about to say so when Kensington Care Home's front door swings opens, and the receptionist comes thumping down the stairs on her white, rubber-soled shoes. As she gets closer, I realize she's put on a fresh coat of bright pink lipstick. She makes a beeline for Gareth. Matthew turns his away so she won't recognize him.

"Excuse me, Doctor." She waves a clipboard. "You and your party forgot to sign out."

"Sorry," says Gareth. "Can I sign out for all of us?"

"Of course." Her cheeks redden as she hands him the board with a business card clipped to the top. "That's my card, um, in case you need to contact us regarding your patient."

"He's not my patient. We're just visiting." He holds the board up so she can't see and adds the name Matt Smith before signing us out. He doesn't take the bait. I'm a little disappointed. I was willing to bet good money her personal number was written on the back that card.

She's disappointed, too, along with being clueless she's barking up the wrong tree. She chews her lip, staining her teeth pink as tries to think of something else to say. Gareth holds out the clipboard.

Gunshots bursts through the air. The clipboard flies with sudden force from Gareth's hand. The receptionist screams and runs upstairs. We're about to follow, but there's more gunfire and we duck behind a row of parked cars. Confusion and panic stir the tourists into a frenzy. I can hear them shouting and running. Penny is crouched beside me.

"You okay?" I ask, even though I'm pretty sure I'd feel it if she were hurt.

"Yeah. You?"

I'm about to answer when more gunfire blazes. We duck,

huddling into each other. Windows shatter. Penny closes her eyes and holds out her hand. Glass slices through the air, falling all around us, but not on us as the energy of the Yin Pearl surrounds us in a protective bubble.

Can that stop bullets? I ask her.

Maybe, but not for long.

Do you need help?

Not right now. Save your energy.

The shooting stops. I doubt he's done. Maybe he's reloading. Maybe he's waiting for people to run so he can pick them off.

Gareth presses his phone to his ear and listens before speaking. "A sniper made it to the roof of a hotel. Our guards can't get to him. Hotel security won't let them inside."

I take a deep breath to ease the flow of adrenaline pumping through my body. Dragon energy shrinks with fear and roars with anger. That's why dragons are cold, so they can control their flow of energy and use it to their best advantage. I need to do the same. Be cold and calm and consider the best strategy, which is to stop the sniper. The only way to do that is the Dragon Shout, but I don't know where he is or how to reach him... No. Panic thoughts don't help. I take another breath, allowing the icy dragon energy to flow through my veins. The pinprick at my chest sharpens, activating the Yang Pearl and amplifying its power.

Penny's mind brushes mine. *Can I help?*

Yeah. I pause. *I'm going to kill him.*

Let's do it.

I feel the icy energy flowing through her and don't ask if she's sure.

We join hands as the sniper starts shooting again. Matthew tries to cover Penny, but she pushes him gently away. Everything dims as the energy of the Yin Pearl flows through me into the Yang Pearl. I thought the energy would feel pure and healing, but this is war and what comes is pure dragon, cold-blooded and favoring logic over mercy. I sense an energy bubble forming around us, combining the flow of our *chi* through our pearls. I reach out my left hand and release the Dragon Shout.

I send the energy not in front of me, but above, across the street, seeking out the sniper, drawn like a magnet to his dark aura and bad karma. He stops shooting as he senses our energy coiling around him. He stiffens, the automatic rifle falling from hands as he starts struggling, trying to break free. His strangled voice cries out as his heart pounds. I can feel every beat. It makes me feel powerful and horrible as my fingers curl and I yank him over the edge of the building. He's falling, screaming, and I cut the connection so we don't feel him die.

For a second, everything is silent. Relief flows through us. The connection fades until we are two separate people, squeezing the hell out of each other's hand.

Sirens blare and screams intensify. Hysteria and self-preservation have gripped the crowd and people are running in all directions. I'm tugged to my feet by Gareth. My legs buckle. The energy from Jade Dragon has been sapped, leaving me weak and limp as a rag. Matthew lifts Penny, keeping his arms around her for support.

"Can you move?" asks Gareth.

She and I both nod. I lean heavily on him as he half drags me across the square. Panicked people rush past us, shoving everyone out of their way, separating us from Penny and Matthew. Gareth and I stop so they can catch up. A wall of bodies slams into us. Gareth wraps his arms around me as I lose my footing. Pain spikes in my twisting ankle. I cling to him and manage to stay upright. I wonder if he realizes he's saving the son of the man who killed Gerry. Would he dump me on the ground if he knew?

"All right?" he asks.

I test my ankle and nod as Penny and Matthew rejoin us. We plough ahead, reaching the park just as armored police come storming through, shields in one hand, automatic rifles in the other. Gareth tugs me toward the shelter of a hotel awning. Penny and Matthew follow. We huddle there while the cops spread out, eying everyone as potential suspects or victims. Luckily, the fleeing Korean tourists make me and Matthew appear less obvious.

Gareth surveys the scene before yelling above the noise, "Forget the mail train. We'll go to Paddington Station."

Emergency vehicles clog the street as they pull up next to the park. Crowds of people stand in front of buildings and store fronts, eager for a view but ready to bolt inside at the first sign of trouble. We peal out of the doorway and ride the wave of frantic bodies, past the battalion of cops, all the way to the station. The turnstiles are jammed with people fleeing the scene and it takes a while to get through. The narrow platform is packed with people desperate to get on the train. With so many people, we can't talk freely. Gareth glances all around, seeking out any enemies who might've followed us.

All right? asks Penny.

Yeah. You?

Yeah.

We share a moment, the warmth of connection, but it breaks as the overhead sign lights up, indicating an approaching train.

It pulls into the station. The doors open and it's a mad scramble as people fight to get on board. The four of us surge forward. Elbows and shoulders knock me around and I shove back, trying to get through. Although it's cold outside, everyone down here is sweating and reeking of fear. Penny and Matthew board first. Gareth and I are right behind, but the car is too full and the bloat of bodies sends us back onto the platform. Penny and Matthew struggle to rejoin us, but the doors slide shut, and the train takes off.

"Shit," I cry out.

"Bugger," says Gareth. He pulls out his phone. "I'll call Helena."

Penny

Helena stays on the phone with me, and I follow her instructions as Matthew and I exit the train. The majority of passengers are also getting off here, most of them still edgy about the "terrorist attack." Wild rumors are already flying, with the gunman being called a terrorist. I feel edgy, too, for a different reason. Lennon and I are stronger together than apart, and we still have targets on our backs. I won't feel safe until we're together again.

We head down a corridor to where a trio of ragged buskers are playing a cover of the Black Eyed Peas' "I Gotta Feeling." Helena stands beside them, cane resting on her shoulder while she scans the jostling crowd. Her pixie-like features freeze with shock as she spots us. Then her hand flies to her mouth when we stand before her. Tears fill her eyes.

"I can't believe it," she whispers. Her hands cup Matthew's face. "It's really you."

"It's really me," he whispers back hoarsely. "God, Helena, the coma. It feels like forever, but it also feels like I just saw you."

My heart swells as they embrace. Matthew is reclaiming his

life. It's not the one he once had, but it's so much better than the purgatory to which his parents had condemned him.

The pinprick needles my chest. Something isn't right. Using the Yin Pearl. I cast through the crowd for danger.

And find it.

A man dressed in dark clothes, sunglasses, and black knit cap is closing in on us. My impending murder colors his energy, making him radiate dark red. The corridor is too brightly lit for him to use the Stealth Skill, so he uses the crowd for cover instead. If I were at full power, I'd drain his life force, the same way I had the Wongs, but as it is, I can barely stand. What can I do with my depleted energy? Instinctively, I reach for Helena, gripping her arm. She lets go of Matthew and stares at me, startled.

"See him," I whisper as I pour the pearl's vision into her.

Her face goes blank. She blinks several times. Then her eyes brighten with a sort of frenzy and she tilts back her head to howl with laughter. She tugs away from me like a child from a mother, and twirls around, swinging her cane and dancing to the music with sloppy, swaying steps. Slurring the lyrics in a loud voice, she sways into the crowd. People curse and glare while dodging past her and her cane. Someone shoves her away, and she uses the momentum to slam into the assassin, knocking him against the wall. He attempts to shove her away, but then freezes. Helena has twisted the handle off of her cane and is pressing the revolver end into his side.

Matthew and I rush over to give her more cover. She hands Matthew her cane, reaches into the man's waistband, and pulls out a gun which she shoves into one of her skirt's numerous pockets. His dark red energy rages. As soon as we retreat, he'll go at us again with whatever skills he has. He wants me dead and will achieve that goal, whatever the cost. I exchange tense glances with Helena. She feels it, too.

There's a pop as she pulls the trigger and her arm recoils

slightly. The man bends over, grasping his side. She steps away, allowing him to scarper away into the clueless crowd. I check our clothes for blood spatter, but she's too skilled for that.

"Won't the police notice a dead body?" I ask in a breathless whisper.

She shrugs as she reattaches the gun to her cane. "This antique won't kill him. Not if he gets to a doctor in time."

"But…" I glance up at the overhead cameras.

She gently shakes her head as if I'm being thick. "Off. We'll turn them back on as soon as we leave, which is to say right now."

I couldn't agree more. I try reaching out to Lennon, but my energy is once again exhausted. "We need to warn Gareth and Lennon."

"I will," she says. "Don't worry. They'll be well guarded as soon as they're off the train and Gareth knows the tunnels. Let's go."

What I want to do is go back to the platform and wait for them, but Matthew and I are surrounded by Mad Maud and the buskers and hustled into the Clan's labyrinth below.

Lennon

While Gareth talks to Maud, I double over, pressing my hands into my thighs, and gulping foul air as a wave of dizziness passes through me. He grabs hold of me so I don't get jostled off the ledge. I have to put my arm across his shoulders and lean into him for support.

He hangs up and glances around before speaking in my ear. "Helena's taking care of them. Are you okay?"

I take a deep breath. "I will be in a moment."

I feel the tension in his body. Is it because he doesn't like me? Or is it because he's a gay man with a kid hanging all over him? I mean, no one knows he's gay, but I get it. I know what it's like having people be hypercritical and judge my every move. It makes you self-conscious, until you decide you don't give a fuck.

By the time the next train comes, I'm able to get aboard and stand on my own since all the seats are taken. I reach out, seeking Penny's energy, but she's too far and I'm too weak. I concentrate instead on the pinprick burning in my chest. The dragon energy is still there. I close my eyes and sway with the motion of the train, focusing solely on that energy, allowing it to spread through my body and strengthen my *chi*.

I don't know how much time passes before Gareth shakes my shoulder and says, "Next station."

I exhale, but don't relax. I'm strong enough to face whatever's thrown at me, and I know it's going to be a lot, including Mad Maud demanding answers I can't give. She and her brother will want to shove me outside when they find out what my father did. Want to but can't since they need me alive.

Two Beggars are waiting for us on the platform. Both are wearing green Hearth jackets, bulky enough to hide an arsenal of concealed weapons. They escort us away from the crowd and into the service corridors, until we reach a door marked, "No Entry for Unauthorized Personnel." Gareth taps his card to the reader and the two of us enter. The lights automatically flicker on, revealing a small, windowless room, empty except for another door, also marked the same.

"No one suspects anything?" I ask as he presses his card to that reader.

He gives a small, grim laugh. "Bureaucracy is our greatest ally."

Funny how that's true everywhere.

The opened door leads to a winding metal staircase that seems to go down forever. We finally reach the bottom and head along a narrow walkway through a dimly lit tunnel. I get the sense we're deeper than in Gray Coat Station. The air is thicker, and the tunnels are constructed with oily limestone bricks and rusted iron arches with huge rivets. The track below is covered in dust and rat shit, and I can't help shuddering when I see a few of them skitter along the rail. Finally, we reach a nameless platform that looks pre-20th Century. On its tracks sits a wood-paneled train attached to a steam engine. My mouth drops open. It looks like something from a museum or a movie.

"That got left down here?"

"You wouldn't believe what got left down here." Gareth doesn't elaborate. He slides open the door to the first car.

I don't step inside. "Who lives here?"

"No one. This train is for special occasions and guests."

Or for keeping someone you don't want around. "Where's Penny?"

"With her father."

"Not here."

"No." He takes a breath. "Matthew told me what happened to him and Gerry. I'm not surprised. Your father was a prick."

My shoulders tense. Shit. Here we go again.

"We were introduced at Helena's first Beggars' Banquet. Not a problem. Later, when I walked by him and his brother, I heard him say, 'That's Maud's queer brother.' And your uncle asked, 'Does he have AIDS?' And they both laughed. I'd just gotten home after being wounded in Afghanistan."

My teeth clench so tight, my jaw aches. This is so not fair. Why do his crimes have to bite me in the ass?

"Later in the evening, your father came up to me. He'd been in his cups, so I expected the worst. He told me I should move to San Francisco, that it's easier to be gay there, and that he'd put in a good word for me with John Walks Long."

"What did you say?"

"I told him I'd overheard the two of them and I challenged him."

My eyes widen. That was ballsy.

"I knew I didn't have a chance in hell with him. I wanted the opportunity to punch him in the face and I told him as much." He sucks in his breath. "Your father bowed his head and said he accepted and conceded. I'd won and was welcome to tell anyone. Then he walked away."

My throat aches because that sounds like the Dad I knew, strong, but also humble. He was in no danger of losing command of the Crossroads either way, since informal challenges don't count toward that, but still.

Gareth's lips press tight. "God, I hated him for that. I still do. And now I learn he killed Gerry."

Tears fill my eyes. I choke out, "I'm so sorry."

He shrugs. "I don't blame you. You seem an all right sort. I'm telling you all this for one reason. Stay away from Penny. I don't know what magic you two are working together, but you need to let her go. Find someone else."

"My own kind?" I spit that out because he knows what it's like to be ostracized for who he loves.

"I didn't say that. It's not about that. It's about keeping her safe. You've nothing but trouble to offer her."

"I healed Matthew."

"That you did and we thank you." There's no gratitude in his tone. "We'll make arrangements so you can fly out of here. When you get back to San Francisco, let her go."

We stare at each other and I look away first because macho Crossroads bullshit doesn't fly with me. I step inside the car and slide the door shut. Then I sit on the padded red velvet bench and stare at the ornate wooden walls. It was definitely meant for someone who travels in style. I lean back and close my eyes. This has been the worst/best/strangest day of my entire life. I don't know how to face the future. Right now, I can only handle having one goal: stopping Uncle George.

I close my eyes, reaching out from within, and feel the gossamer thread connecting me to Penny for as long as we both wear the pearls. I give it a little tug and it vibrates as her mind touches mine.

Hey, we're here, at the Abode, she says. *Where are you?*

The dungeon.

Lol. No, really.

Really. I don't know where I am. They want to keep us apart. Can you blame them?

There's a silence even though we're still connected. There's more I want to say, bubbling up in me like a toxic stew, about to overflow if I don't turn down the heat.

This isn't your fault, she says. *And trying to make it your fault won't help anything.*

I sigh, letting the steam escape. *I know, I guess, but if feels like it is.*

Well, it's not. She pauses. *All these people, they don't know you, not like I do.*

The sludge in my soul slows to a simmer. Maybe everyone else hates me, but she doesn't. I can't give up the Yang Pearl if it means giving up this connection to the one person who understands me.

I'll find you, she says.

I know.

I do know because that's what people don't understand about us. We always find each other in the end.

We're taken to the same carriage, but this time I don't mind because Gerry is waiting there for us. I sense his joy as he wraps his ghostly arms around his best mate. Matthew stops in his tracks and sucks in his breath. His eyes become sad with longing.

"Are you all right?" asks Helena.

He wipes his hand across his face. "Yeah… I was just… thinking about Gerry."

I open my mouth and close it again while Gerry wafts near me. *No, love. Don't.* His voice is faint, as if he's barely here.

I know. I won't. He's been through enough.

Helena calls my mother and hands the phone to Matthew.

"Bridie?" Tears fill his eyes. He whispers hoarsely, "Yes, it's really me, love."

Gerry presence pulses, becoming strong and joyous, before fading again. He's nearly gone after holding on so long for this moment. There's something I have to ask him.

Da, why didn't you tell me Lennon's father killed you?

What good would that've done? You needed the lad to save Matthew.

What about now that Matthew's saved?

I can almost see him wink. *Follow your heart, Penny Lane. I'd never tell you otherwise.*

Helena tugs my arm and pulls me aside. "I heard back from my people in the square, about how the sniper was somehow pushed off the roof. I assume the Dragon Son used his powers. Back at the station, though, you warned me somehow. What did you do?"

This is the moment I've been dreading. I respect Mad Maud too much to sham her with false ignorance or a cock-and-bull tale. Only the truth will do, and since I can't give her that, all I can say is, "I can't tell you."

She folds her arms. "You have to choose sides, Penny."

Something of Gerry triggers in me, reminding me I'm his daughter. I tilt my head along with my smile. "With respect, I don't. I walk the Wayward Way. Always have. Always will."

"So, you're choosing the Two Dragon Clan."

"I'm choosing to help my friend. Helping him helps you."

She shakes her head. "This isn't a game. This is real life with adult consequences."

I look at Matthew as I say, "I know."

Gareth enters. A smile lights his face, but the glow soon fades from his eyes. I know he doesn't begrudge Bridie and Matthew their joy, but, oh, how he wishes it was him. He sinks into a chair and closes his eyes as Gerry's waning spirit wraps around him. Maud sits beside him and takes his hand. For a moment, I can almost picture them all as they were when they were young. Do they still see themselves that way? I know they still see me as a child in need of protection. Only Gerry understands me, and he's almost gone. I don't want to be here when he fades away. I turn away.

Bye, Da. I love you.

I love you, Penny Lane. His reply is so faint, I feel rather than hear it.

I won't cry. I'm done with tears. All that matters now is action. The only justice I can seek is with the son of Gerry's killer. The boy I love.

I slip outside and concentrate on that love, following the silvery thread that connects me to Lennon for as long as I wear the Yin Pearl.

I don't want to be stopped and questioned. Even as I think that, a glow of dragon energy surrounds me, allowing me to glide past the guards unnoticed. How powerful are these pearls? Is that why no one wants me and Lennon together, because they don't trust us with this power, because we're disobedient, unpredictable kids?

I smile. They're right. They shouldn't trust us. Lennon and I have our own agenda and now, no one can stop us.

The story continues in Spawn: Dragons of the Crossroads Book 4. Penny and Lennon return to San Francisco, pursued by their enemies, and feared by their clans for the power they wield. Dark magic will be unleashed, and hidden truths revealed as they battle a brutal enemy who can only be defeated if their divided families come together.

To find out more about Dragons of the Crossroads and to purchase more books in the series, please go to loriwriter.com.

Acknowledgments

Heartfelt thanks to my editors: Jennifer Gagliardi and India
Cale.

Thank you to Genine Tyson and Deb McIntyre for organizing
the weekly Shut Up and Write Marathon where much of this
book was written.

Shout-out to the San Francisco Bay Area Indie Authors group
for all the great advice.

About the Author

Lori Saltis left her heart in San Francisco. She goes to visit it whenever she can afford the bridge toll. She's been an indie author since 2016. She's very passionate about the themes of alienation and found family. Her favorite genre is fantasy because who doesn't want to believe they'll look up in the sky one day and see a dragon?

To find out more about the world of the Crossroads, check out her website loriwriter.com.

www.ingramcontent.com/pod-product-compliance
Lightning Source LLC
Chambersburg PA
CBHW020759310726
48969CB00002B/609